BULLWHIPPED!

Black Elk rode forward, turned his pony, and raised his whip. "You squaw-stealing dog," he said in a voice meant just for Touch the Sky's ears. "Your hot blood will cool once it drips into the plains!"

Again and again Black Elk brought his whip down, opening up lacerations all over Touch the Sky's body. Only when Black Elk's arm began to tire did the other warriors set upon him.

"Cry, Woman Face!" Wolf Who Hunts Smiling taunted Touch the Sky, breathing heavily from his exertions with the whip.

A moment later Wolf Who Hunts Smiling leaped back in rage when Touch the Sky hawked up a wad of phlegm and spat it into his face.

"Wolf Who Hunts Smiling!" Touch the Sky cried. "I warn you, best to kill me now or I will turn your guts into worm fodder...."

6 CHEYENNE

COMANCHE RAID
JUDD COLE

LEISURE BOOKS **NEW YORK CITY**

A LEISURE BOOK®

July 1993

Published by

Dorchester Publishing Co., Inc.
276 Fifth Avenue
New York, NY 10001

Printed in the United States of America.

Prologue

In 1840 Running Antelope and his Northern Cheyenne band were massacred by blue-bloused pony soldiers. The only survivor was his infant son.

His Cheyenne name lost forever, the boy was adopted by John and Sarah Hanchon and raised in the Wyoming Territory settlement of Bighorn Falls. They named him Matthew and loved him as if he were their own blood.

For a long time their love was enough to protect him from the hatred other settlers felt for a full-blooded Indian in their midst. But then he turned 16 and fell in love with Kristen Steele, who returned his love. Her father had the youth viciously beaten. Knowing he was as good as dead unless he left her alone, Kristen lied and told

5

Matthew she didn't want to see him anymore.

Then a young cavalry officer named Seth Carlson, who planned to marry Kristen, threatened to ruin John and Sarah Hanchon's mercantile business unless Matthew cleared out for good. Forsaken in love, driven from the white man's world to save his parents, he fled north to the Powder River and Cheyenne country.

He was suspected of being a spy, and the Cheyenne nearly killed him. He was considered no better than a white man's dog by most of Chief Yellow Bear's tribe. But Arrow Keeper, the tribe shaman, had recently experienced a powerful medicine vision. This tall youth was marked by destiny to become a great warrior and leader of his people, though much suffering must come first.

Though Matthew was renamed Touch the Sky and began to learn the Cheyenne Way, his enemies were many. The fierce young warrior Black Elk hated him instantly when he saw that Chief Yellow Bear's daughter, Honey Eater, was captivated by the tall stranger. And Black Elk's younger cousin, Wolf Who Hunts Smiling, openly announced his intention to kill the suspected spy.

After helping to save his tribe from annihilation by Pawnees, Touch the Sky earned some respect and trust from the Headmen. But his enemies hated him even more for this recognition. Then Henri Lagace and his whiskey traders invaded Indian country, kidnapping Honey Eater when Chief Yellow Bear's tribe painted for war against them. Touch the Sky killed Lagace and freed Honey Eater. But now, after hearing Honey Eater swear her love for Touch the Sky, Black Elk hated him more than ever.

The tribe's suspicions against him only deepened when Touch the Sky rushed back to the river-bend settlement of Bighorn Falls to help his white parents. Hiram Steele and Lieutenant Seth Carlson had already ruined the Hanchons' mercantile trade; now they had launched a bloody campaign to drive them from their new mustang spread.

Assisted by his friend Little Horse, Touch the Sky defeated hs parents' enemies. But his tragic plight worsened when he returned to the Cheyenne camp. Chief Yellow Bear had died, forcing Honey Eater to marry Black Elk. Worse, spies watched Touch the Sky during his absence. They mistook his meetings with the sympathetic cavalry officer Tom Riley as proof the Cheyenne was a traitor to his people.

Old Arrow Keeper used his power as acting chief to save the youth. He announced that Touch the Sky would be trained in the shaman arts. He sent the young buck to sacred Medicine Lake in the Black Hills, to seek the same vision that Arrow Keeper had originally experienced. Touch the Sky received the images and secrets of the Vision Path, and saw his destiny as a great warrior who would someday lead the Shaiyena people in one last great victory.

But he knew he must face many dangers before that time arrived. Shortly after his key vision at Medicine Lake, the chief-renewal ceremony was held, and Gray Thunder was selected to replace the dead Chief Yellow Bear.

During the festivities, a keelboat called the *Sioux Princess* sailed into camp. The skipper, Wes Munro, claimed to be on a "goodwill" trip through Indian country, distributing gifts from the Indian Bureau. In fact, he was signing illegal "private treaties" with renegade subchiefs, swindling the tribes out of their best land so he could start a transcontinental wagon road.

Chief Gray Thunder sent Touch the Sky, Little Horse, and their enemy Wolf Who Hunts Smiling to join the crew of the *Sioux Princess* as replacements for boatmen killed in a Mandan raid. They learned of Munro's plans, and worked secretly to thwart him. Captured and brutally tortured, they escaped and brought word to their tribe.

Touch the Sky counted first coup in the climactic battle against Munro's mercenaries. But the jealous Black Elk hated him more than ever after catching Honey Eater crying in fear for Touch the Sky's safety on the keelboat. And the ambitious Wolf Who Hunts Smiling, who dreamed of leading the tribe in a war against the Bluecoat pony soldiers, had warned Touch the Sky that one of them must die.

Chapter 1

In the Moon When the Ponies Shed, Chief Gray
Thunder of the Northern Cheyenne sent out
scouts to locate buffalo trails. The cold moons
had been long and hard, and the tribe badly
needed fresh meat.

The scouts returned with welcome news. The
fresh trail of a huge herd had been spotted in
the Valley of the Greasy Grass, near the Little
Bighorn. It led due south toward the Colorado
Plains.

The Cheyenne Hunt Law was strict on the matter of buffalo hunting. Because buffalo were so
essential to Cheyenne survival, and because everyone was needed if waste was to be avoided, the
entire tribe must take part in the annual buffalo
hunts.

The unusually harsh winter had kept most of the tribe huddled around the firepits in their tipis. Now, with the new grass well up and the mountain runoff swelling the rivers and creeks, the entire tribe was ready for the welcome activity of the hunt. The Headmen did not even bother to count stones when they voted on Gray Thunder's proposal to head south in pursuit of the buffalo.

Touch the Sky was even more excited than most of the others. Though he had been on several hunts since joining the tribe nearly four winters ago, in the year white men called 1856, this was the first time the trail had led so far south. They would be traveling to the lands of tribes he had seldom seen—not only their brothers, the Southern Cheyennes, and their allies, the Southern Arapahos, but enemy tribes too, as Arrow Keeper reminded him.

"The new soldiertowns erected by the Bluecoats," the old shaman explained, "have sent up the white man's stink, frightening the herds and turning them far to the south. Now we must approach the valleys and peaks of the Kiowa and their loyal battle companions, the Comanches."

Touch the Sky listened eagerly as he lashed tipi covers to a packhorse. He and the elder were standing just inside a huge corral formed by buffalo-hair ropes snubbed around cottonwood trees. It was the custom for every member of the tribe past infancy to perform work related to the hunt. But since Touch the Sky had no official clan to designate his task, Arrow Keeper had assigned this one. No one questioned this openly, since Arrow Keeper was the most respected elder in the tribe. And Touch the Sky was, after all, his apprentice in the shaman arts—a fact which caused several to remark privately that old Arrow Keeper had gone soft in his brain.

"The Kiowa," Arrow Keeper said, "are the envy of the red nations, for their pony herds are the finest. Better even than our Shaiyena ponies, and where is the Bluecoat horse that can match ours? But it is the fierce Comanche who truly become one with a horse! I swear by the sun and the earth I live on—there are no finer horsemen anywhere."

Touch the Sky nodded as he used rawhide thongs to secure the buffalo-hide tipi covers. He had nearly 20 winters behind him and was tall and broad-shouldered for a Cheyenne. The days had warmed since the spring melt, and now he wore only a clout, buckskin leggings, and elkskin moccasins. He had a strong, hawk nose, and his thick black locks were shaggy and long except over his brow. There they had been cropped short to leave his vision unobstructed.

"I have seen Comanches when their ponies are shot out from under them," Arrow Keeper said. "They are bowlegged and oddly built, and on foot the most awkward creatures I have ever seen. It is said they lose their courage too when not on horseback. But when riding in battle, there is not a coward among them."

"Father!" a mounted warrior shouted from the clearing in front of the council lodge. "Gray Thunder sent me to ask you. Should the soldier

11

societies prepare for the Animal Dance tonight?"

Arrow Keeper nodded. The young warrior, a member of the Cheyenne military society known as the Bowstrings, raced off to find the camp crier so the word could be spread. Touch the Sky watched the brightly dyed feathers tied to the tail of the warrior's horse. These marked him as a member of a military society, or soldier troop, which had been selected to enforce the rigid Hunt Law between the day of the Animal Dance and the final slaughter of the hunt.

By now Touch the Sky had learned how the various soldier troops differed from each other. The Bowstrings were the favorites because of their belief that negotiating was the best way to end a confrontation. The Bull Whips, in contrast, were quick to resort to their highly feared knotted-thong whips.

Arrow Keeper saw Touch the Sky staring at the dyed feathers.

"Soon, little brother," he said, "you must consider which society you wish to join. I suggest the Bowstrings. Their leader is Spotted Tail of the Eagle Clan. He has courage, but also the good sense to look before he wades in. I cannot say the same for Lone Bear, who heads the Bull Whips."

Touch the Sky nodded. "Little Horse tells me that Wolf Who Hunts Smiling has brought a gift of arrows to Lone Bear. That he wishes to join their society."

"Your friend Little Horse speaks the straight word," Arrow Keeper said. "I am not surprised. Wolf Who Hunts Smiling is hot-tempered and quick to rise up on his hind legs. He will make a good Bull Whip. They are becoming more and more like the Dog Men of the Southern Cheyenne who ride under the leader War Horse. True, they are fearsome warriors to be respected. But they openly defy their Headmen and the chief."

"Will his gift be accepted?" Touch the Sky said. "Will he be initiated?"

Arrow Keeper shrugged. Despite the warming weather, he was still wrapped snugly in his red blanket. His long hair was much thinner than Touch the Sky's, silver and brittle with age.

"He is young, younger even than you. Normally a Cheyenne buck does not go to war before he has sixteen winters behind him. Before he approaches the soldier societies, he should have at least four winters behind him as a warrior. But Wolf Who Hunts Smiling was blooded early, like his cousin Black Elk. He can easily defeat any two Bull Whips, and Lone Bear knows this."

Touch the Sky finished his task in disheartened silence. Wolf Who Hunts Smiling was already doing a good job of keeping many in the tribe suspicious of Touch the Sky. How arrogant and influential would he be once initiated into the fierce Bull Whip Society?

Arrow Keeper reminded Touch the Sky that he would be needed to assist at the Animal Dance later. When the old shaman returned to his tipi to rest, Touch the Sky took a break from his boring labors to check on his ponies.

While he headed toward the far end of the corral, threading his way through the grazing ponies, he thought again of the upcoming hunt. Despite the dangers of entering enemy territory, the risk must be taken. Gray Thunder's Cheyenne people needed much more from the buffalo than just fresh and jerked meat. They were critically short on hides for tipi covers, on warm fur sleeping robes and winter leggings. Cups would be made from the horns, belts and ropes from the hair, thread from the sinews, water bags from the bladders.

Touch the Sky paused to watch a mare frisking with her new foal. Overhead, a red-tailed hawk circled against a seamless blue sky. Down by the river, a badger was digging its burrow. Wildflowers were ablaze further out on the prairie, and the rivers and creeks were swollen with snow runoff. The snowcapped mountain peaks on the horizon glittered white in the bright sunlight.

One of Touch the Sky's earliest lessons among the Cheyennes was to talk and think less and observe more. And lately, at Arrow Keeper's quiet but steady urging, his young shaman apprentice was developing the habit of reading the secret language of nature. This very morning, Arrow Keeper had shown him how to examine a spider's web and predict whether the warm moons would be rainy or dry—long, thin threads meant dry weather, short and fat meant rainy. This particular web had foretold a rainy summer, good news since it meant the buffalo grass would be high and the herds fat.

Touch the Sky spotted a beautiful gray pony with a thick white mane, stamping her feet in irritation at pesky flies. He cut her from the herd. She nuzzled his shoulder, glad to see him again. He had stolen her from a Crow warrior after beating Wolf Who Hunts Smiling at counting first coup on him.

Touch the Sky grabbed a handful of mane. He was about to swing up onto his pony when a familiar voice abruptly caught his attention. Clearly the speaker was infuriated.

"You make me a squaw in front of my clan brothers! I have warned you before about doing your duty!"

Black Elk! Touch the Sky peered over his pony's withers. The river was close by, and the grass dipped sharply to form its bank. So at first he spotted only Black Elk's muscle-corded back. The young war chief was speaking to someone further down the bank, out of sight.

"This is proof you do not carry my son in your womb! Why do you not bathe with the others? It is because your belly-mouth bleeds the unclean blood!"

Suddenly Touch the Sky understood he must be speaking to Honey Eater. Cheyenne women were required to bathe separately when their bleeding time came.

"You make me a squaw!" he repeated angrily. "The others are joking behind my back, saying that perhaps a Pawneee must be brought into my tipi to make a son for me!"

His threatening tone alerted Touch the Sky. The young brave swung under the corral ropes and headed slowly toward the river. Every instinct warned him not to interfere with the fierce Black Elk. Yet those same instincts drew him to protect Honey Eater from his wrath. Now Touch the Sky could hear her speaking.

"I do my duty and submit. You have your pleasure at night. Would you fault me because Maiyun has not chosen to make me a mother yet?"

15

"I am a warrior, I do not quarrel with women! When I speak, you listen! It is common knowledge that, if a squaw hardens her heart toward her buck, his seed will not fertilize. You have turned your heart to stone against me. Thus, you deny me my son!"

"Has Black Elk been visiting the Peyote Soldiers? This is wild nonsense."

"The cow does not bellow to the bull! I swear by the four directions, I will *shame* you into your duty, wife!"

Touch the Sky broke into a run, fear icing his veins, when he saw Black Elk grab his knife from its beaded sheath and leap down the bank. There was a sharp cry of protest from Honey Eater, a snarl of rage from Black Elk. By the time Touch the Sky reached the edge of the bank and peered down, the damage had been done.

Honey Eater was still damp from her bath, and her doeskin dress clung to the soft curves of her body. Sunlight gleamed off the bone choker around her neck. A sob hitched in her chest when Black Elk threw the long, beautiful braid he had just cut off into the churning water of the Powder River.

Rage warred with pity in Touch the Sky's breast. Honey Eater's long, thick hair had been her pride. Every day she picked fresh columbine petals to braid into it. She looked lost and vulnerable now without it, her once-beautiful hair now a mass of jagged locks over her nape. Worse, Touch the Sky knew that cutting off a squaw's braid was a public mark of shame. Black Elk had announced that she was failing to do her duty as a Cheyenne wife. He was calling on

16

public censure by the tribe to force her to her senses.

"Leave me alone!" Honey Eater said bitterly. "I cannot bear to look at your arrogant, accusing face. If I *can* prevent your child from growing in my womb, I surely will. Once I thought you were a hard man, but a fair one. I was wrong, you are only hard."

Black Elk's rage was instant. He lifted his hand to hit her.

Touch the Sky drew his knife and shouted, "Touch her again, and I swear by my medicine bundle I will send you under!"

Black Elk whirled and looked up the bank. Honey Eater too stared at him. Her shame at the public mark of dishonor was evident immediately in the deep flush which turned even her earlobes red.

Black Elk watched the two of them drinking each other in with their eyes. Disgust filled his voice when he said, "Moon Calf and his bitch-in-rut! Did you come down here, Woman Face, hoping to bull my squaw?"

"Only to save her from murder," the tall youth retorted. "The heathen Comanches, Arrow Keeper says, can kill their wives and it is not murder. But the Cheyenne Way does not permit wife-slaughter."

"No, *shaman,*" Black Elk said, his tone ominously low with rage, "but it does permit a war leader to take his wife's braid. This is the second time you have pulled your knife and spoken the he-bear talk to me. I *trained* you, buck!"

"And I learned my lessons. Remember this when you lift your hand to strike Honey Eater."

17

"I will remember it *now,* squaw stealer, and gut you like a rabbit!"

Black Elk unsheathed his knife again, his eyes dark and dangerous. His war face was made even more hideous by the dead, leathery flap where part of an ear had been severed by a Bluecoat saber, then later sewn back on with buckskin thread. Again Black Elk thought of the time he had caught Honey Eater kneeling before Touch the Sky's empty tipi, crying in fear for his safety aboard the white men's keelboat.

Touch the Sky made no move to leap down the bank, though his weapon was still in his hand. Black Elk was halfway up the bank when a shout from camp made both braves look that way.

Touch the Sky's drawn knife had earned the attention of a vigilant Bowstring named Tangle Hair. With the hunt preparations underway, they were patrolling the camp.

Tangle Hair raced over on his jet-black mustang.

"Black Elk! Touch the Sky! Would you sully the Arrows even as your tribe prepares for the hunt?"

Despite their anger, Tangle Hair's words shamed both warriors. According to the Cheyenne Way, the four sacred Medicine Arrows, always protected by Arrow Keeper, must be kept forever sweet and clean. The bloodshed of any Cheyenne stained the Arrows, and thus the entire tribe. When violent emotions were brewing, the thought of the Arrows prevented many fights. It would be an especially serious wrong to the tribe to sully them as a hunt was beginning, thus creating bad medicine to scare off the herds.

Tangle Hair nodded toward Touch the Sky. "I am not surprised to see *this* one brandishing his knife as the hunt begins. He was raised among hair faces and it is said he does not truly respect the red man's ways. But you, Black Elk! You are my war leader! For this very reason, you should be the last to risk bloodshed now!"

His words flew straight-arrow. Even the proud Black Elk, who brooked censure from few men, nodded to admit their truth. Still, his anger at Touch the Sky's interference was great.

"This spy for the long knives has been working his trade again," the war chief said, "only now he spies on me as I discipline my squaw."

"I was not spying," Touch the Sky said hotly. "I saw this brave warrior beating a defenseless woman, and I interfered as any warrior is required to do. The Cheyenne Way does not permit the beating of our women."

By now several more Bowstring soldiers had ridden over to see what was wrong. They conferred among themselves for some time in low voices. This was an awkward matter. The tall youth was right. Yet few Cheyenne braves did not occasionally beat their women. It was a private matter. Still, all could see that Black Elk had cut off Honey Eater's beautiful hair. This was a severe punishment for a girl well liked by everyone in the tribe, the daughter of the great Chief Yellow Bear.

The Bowstrings now demonstrated their tact once again. Clearly, Black Elk's pride had been offended, his manhood challenged publicly by

Touch the Sky's interference. Yet they grudgingly agreed among themselves that the youth had been right to do so.

"Black Elk," said Tangle Hair. "Help us have a good hunt! It has been decided that you should ride over with us now to our troop's pony herd. Select two of our finest ponies and add them to your string. A warrior with so many feathers in his bonnet should have the pick of the best."

The last thing Black Elk needed was more ponies. But Tangle Hair's gesture allowed him to save face without risking the severe stigma of murder. Black Elk nodded. Then he fixed his stone-eyed stare on Touch the Sky and said, "I have no desire to sully the Arrows. But Bow-strings, during this hunt watch this white man's dog close and keep him far from me, or I swear his gut will string my next bow!"

Chapter 2

The Kiowa leader named Hairy Wolf halted his band at the rim of Blanco Canyon.

All around the warrior as far as his eyes could see stretched the vast Llano Estacado, the Staked Plain—a land of endless, barren desert plains divided by sterile mountains and bone-dry arroyos. This remote wilderness, covering much of the Texas Panhandle and eastern New Mexico Territory, was an unsettled, almost treeless wasteland seldom visited by the hair-face whites. It was inhabited by buffalo, antelope, wolves, coyotes, jackrabbits, prairie dogs, rattlesnakes—and the Kiowas' closest allies, the Comanches.

The Llano's searing sunshine and chalky alkali dust made their enemies reluctant to go in pursuit of them—thus it had become the Comanches'

Judd Cole

favorite haunt. Blanco Canyon, the largest single break dividing the Staked Plain, was now home to Iron Eyes and his Quohada, or Antelope Eater, band of Comanche. Hairy Wolf had led his Kiowa warriors from Medicine Lodge Creek in Oklahoma for this important council.

Longtime friends, hunting partners, and battle allies, the Kiowas and Comanches were even closer than the Cheyennes and their Lakota Sioux cousins. Many found this close alliance odd, since the towering, broad-shouldered Kiowa warriors were considered a strikingly handsome tribe; the Comanches, in contrast, were small and bandy-legged and considered homely. Yet in fierce temper and love of battle the two tribes were twins. Both tribes were fluent in Kiowa, Comanche, and Spanish, and used all three languages interchangeably, especially to fool their enemies.

"Painted Lips," Hairy Wolf called to a nearby warrior, "bring me the war pipe."

Painted Lips owned a fine hand-tooled saddle captured during a raid on Mexican soldiers in the Superstition Mountains. He reached into a saddlebag and removed a long clay pipe painted in bright crimson and black. He nudged his pony closer and handed it to his war chief.

Hairy Wolf undid the thongs of a rawhide pouch. He removed a generous pinch of rich white man's tobacco. He stuffed it into the pipe, ready to present to his friend Iron Eyes. It was the custom to always arrive with a pipe filled when recruiting braves for a raid.

"Look!" Painted Lips pointed below into the canyon.

Comanche Raid

Hairy Wolf watched a magnificent herd of ponies suddenly round a sandstone shoulder. The Comanches, like the Kiowas, were rich in horses—indeed, much of their constant fighting with other tribes was to protect, or get back, their herds.

Below, a Comanche herd guard had spotted the Kiowas. He raised his skull-cracker—the stone war club so deadly in the hands of a mounted Comanche—in greeting.

Hairy Wolf lifted his streamered lance high overhead to return the greeting. The Kiowa leader wore captured Bluecoat trousers and boots. He was bare from the waist up except for a bone breastplate. He was huge—well over six feet—and thickly muscled, with an aquiline nose and long, flowing black hair that fell well below his waist. Now it was matted from exposure to pale alkali dust.

Hairy Wolf led his band down the narrow and rock-strewn trail which descended into the canyon. As they drew closer to the bottom, the well-disguised camp began to emerge from its natural camouflage. Unlike the tipis preferred by the northern Plains tribes, Iron Eyes' Comanches lived in one-room, mesquite-branch huts called jacals and in even cruder wickiups—curved-brush shelters which withstood the strong wind and dust storms of the Llano better than tipis.

Iron Eyes had already stepped out of his lodge to meet his Kiowa brothers. Hairy Wolf dismounted and greeted him with a strong bear hug, lifting the smaller Comanche clear off the ground.

Then, still without speaking a word, he solemnly offered Iron Eyes the filled pipe.

The Quohada leader stared at the pipe with the deep-brown eyes characteristic of his people. He had a sun-darkened, oval face. His hair was shorter than Hairy Wolf's, parted exactly in the center and just long enough to brush behind his ears.

"So," Iron Eyes said at last, speaking in the Kiowa tongue, "you are riding into battle. Hair faces?"

Hairy Wolf shook his head as the rest of his warriors dismounted and greeted old friends with their hearty bear hugs.

"Cheyennes," he said.

A look of satisfaction settled on Iron Eyes' weather-seamed but still-youthful face. The Cheyenne tribe had long been bitterly hated by the Kiowas and Comanches. More than 20 winters earlier, the Cheyennes had met their southern enemies in a major battle at Wolf Creek. The Cheyennes had not only possessed muskets and outnumbered their opponents, but had stunned them with their reckless bravery. On that fateful day scores of good Kiowa and Comanche warriors had been sent to the Land Beyond the Sun forever. Even today the words "Remember Wolf Creek!" were a Kiowa-Comanche battle cry which inspired heroism.

Iron Eyes reached out and accepted the pipe. "It was the Cheyenne who sent out the first warrior," he said. "We only sent out the second. Since Wolf Creek, they have constantly stolen our ponies, and for camp fires they have burned our lodges. I hate them almost as much as I hate the hair-mouthed Texans who are stealing our best lands. Come inside and let us smoke this good tobacco while you speak more on this thing."

Comanche Raid

The inside of the jacal was more spacious than the other lodges. The mesquite-branch walls were chinked with red clay. The skin of a roadrunner, the good luck charm of the Comanches, hung from the ceiling. Dangling all around it were enemy scalps. These had been cured and painted bright colors, the hair dyed in bright greens and yellows.

Iron Eyes waited respectfully until Hairy Wolf had seated himself first on a stack of coyote furs. After all, the Kiowa was a member of his tribe's most elite warrior society, the Kaitsenko—the ten bravest warriors of the Kiowa Nation.

They smoked, filling the jacal with the rich smell of the tobacco. Then Hairy Wolf laid the pipe down between them.

"You know," he said, "that the Northern Cheyenne have chosen a brave named Gray Thunder as their new chief?"

Iron Eyes nodded. "He is a good warrior, not so old as their former chief, Yellow Bear."

"He is leading his tribe on the spring hunt. We know this thing because buffalo scouts from his tribe have followed the herds south, close to our ranges. This can only mean they are leaving soon for the annual hunt."

Again Iron Eyes nodded, waiting for more. Outside the hut, a pistol shot, followed by a woman's scream, suddenly rose above the hubbub of voices. Both leaders calmly ignored it. The scream was followed by a loud chorus of laughter.

"You know," Hairy Wolf said, "that Cheyenne Hunt Law requires them to hunt the buffalo as an entire tribe?"

Iron Eyes began to see which direction his friend was grazing. His thin lips eased into a smile. "Of course. They are a people ruled by many strict and foolish laws."

"Yes—and a people whose beautiful women and children command a good price in Santa Fe."

Iron Eyes liked the sound of this. His tribe, like Hairy Wolf's, needed whiskey and new rifles. Both tribes were active in the Comanchero trade conducted with New Mexicans and Mexicans, supplying Indian captives as slaves in exchange for firearms and alcohol. It was illegal, as was slavery itself in both Mexico and the New Mexico Territory. But a constant market for cheap labor and prostitutes made it very profitable—much more so than selling hides or even fine horses. Hides and horses required much time and work, and besides, who wanted to part with a good pony once it was broken right?

"They are too strong in their camp," Hairy Wolf said. "But the tribe will be vulnerable on the move. Especially in a region less familiar to them."

"How far south must they come?"

"Well below the Smoky Hill River. That is the soonest they could catch the herds. We would not have far to ride."

"We can attack," Iron Eyes said, "while the braves are engaged in the hunt. The women and children will be alone at the hunt camp behind the herds."

Again outside there were more sharp cracks from a pistol, and again a woman's scream was followed by a loud ripple of laughter. Again the two war leaders ignored it.

"Brother," Iron Eyes added, "you saw me smoke your pipe. My lips touched it. You are a member of the Kaitsenko, honored by my tribe fully as much as yours. And we Comanche, are we not called the Red Raiders of the Plains? Again our two tribes will ride to battle as one, and the Cheyenne will pay dearly for their victory dance after Wolf Creek."

Hairy Wolf nodded. "We can expect a bloody fight if we do not strike quickly. Their war chief is a young buck named Black Elk, whose coup feathers trail to the ground. He is no warrior to take lightly."

"There is another," Iron Eyes said. "He is even younger. A tall one whom the Pawnee speak of with fear in their voices. They say his medicine is strong, his war lance unerring. They say he can summon insane white men from the forests, conjure up the angry silvertip bear to save himself."

"The Pawnee!" Hairy Wolf said scornfully. "They are fierce warriors, true. But brother, their superstition knows no bounds. Let him summon a crazy white—Hairy Wolf will scalp a soft-brain as quickly as any other hair face!"

"Well said, Kaitsenko! Then we ride north! Human flesh is not only valuable—it need not be broken like horses."

From outside, more pistols shots, more screams.

This time Iron Eyes smiled as he caught his companion's eye. "The ones we plan to *sell* need not be broken," he corrected himself.

Outside the jacal, while the two leaders planned their strike against Gray Thunder's Cheyennes,

27

the braves from both tribes had gathered for the usual festivities when meeting after a long separation.

Whiskey was in short supply. But the Comanches had learned how to make corn beer from the Navajos to the west. There had been the usual competition in riding skills, won, as always, by the Comanches. A brave named Big Tree won shouts of approval from both tribes when he shot 20 arrows and rode 300 yards in the time it took a Kiowa to reload and fire a carbine twice.

But the real entertainment was provided by an Apache squaw the Comanches had captured during a raid into Sonora.

The Comanches prided themselves on having killed more white settlers than any other tribe. Like the Pawnee, they were fond of attacking at night. They excelled at stealth, and were fonder than most tribes of taking captives. And like their battle brothers, the Kiowa, they enjoyed torture—especially of women.

Two Comanche braves named Dog Fat and Standing Feather were in charge of the entertainment. This Apache squaw was too old to fetch much at the auction block and too ugly for the braves to bother rutting on. She was good only for fun.

They had tied a plaited thong around her arms and drawn her hands behind her. They had tied them so tight they turned purple. Then they had tied another thong around her ankles and drawn her feet and hands together. They then had flipped her on her face so she was unable to move, and begun beating on her head with their bows.

Comanche Raid

Her screams were piteous. To add to the torment, they laid their pistols right up against her skull and fired them. The caps and powder flew into her face and hair, producing bruises and powder burns until she was sorely disfigured.

This went on for hours, well into the evening. Now and then someone would throw a rock at her, cracking a rib or fracturing a facial bone. Finally, they grew tired of their sport and wandered off to eat, then sleep.

But the old squaw was still conscious, still begging them to kill her and end the pain. It was Dog Fat who returned, holding a lethally honed bone-handle knife. Casually, he wrenched the Apache's mouth open and reached far into her throat, slicing her tongue out at the very root. He left it lying in the dirt in front of her so she could see it.

She could no longer scream—she was too busy gagging in her body's reflexive effort not to drown in her own blood. This went on for nearly an hour longer before she finally lost the struggle and died.

Chapter 3

"Brother," Little Horse said, "I have heard a thing."

Touch the Sky looked up from the elkskin moccasins he was stitching with a bone awl and sinew thread. He sat beside the cooking tripod outside his tipi. Lost deep in thoughts about the upcoming hunt, he had not heard his friend approaching. All around the two braves, young boys fashioned travois out of limbs and vines, anticipating huge loads of fresh buffalo meat and hides.

"Sit and speak this thing," Touch the Sky told his friend.

Little Horse still moved a bit stiffly as a result of a leg injury inflicted when he was a prisoner aboard the white men's keelboat. He sat beside his friend.

Comanche Raid

"You know that Wolf Who Hunts Smiling wishes to be initiated as a Bull Whip?"

Touch the Sky nodded. His mouth was a grim, determined slit. That was one of the things he had been thinking about when Little Horse walked up. "I know that he has taken the gift of arrows to their leader, Lone Bear."

"He has," Little Horse said. "But do you also know that Black Elk is changing over to the Bull Whips?"

"But he is a Bowstring!"

"Lately he has told certain braves that he is not happy with Spotted Tail and his Bowstring troop. He claims that the Bowstrings settle things too much like women, that they are afraid to punish those who violate the Cheyenne Way. Also, Spotted Tail preaches cooperation with the pale-faces who can be trusted. Lone Bear is for the warpath against all of them. Black Elk has ears for such talk."

"Yes," Touch the Sky said, "like his cousin, Wolf Who Hunts Smiling."

Touch the Sky said nothing about the incident earlier when Black Elk had cut off Honey Eater's braid. But Black Elk had accepted the Bow-strings' ponies, and now he had openly turned his back on them! Touch the Sky knew full well the reason behind Black Elk's hardening of heart. It was the fact that Honey Eater loved *him*, a Cheyenne who had been raised by whites, instead of Black Elk.

"Hearing this hurt my ears," Little Horse said. "The Bull Whips have many enemies among the tribe, those who believe in ways besides harsh punishment to settle disputes. Black Elk is a

31

respected warrior, chosen battle chief over many older braves. By joining Lone Bear's troop, he lends the strength of his many coups to the name and beliefs of the Bull Whips."

"And the strength of his coups to Wolf Who Hunts Smiling's request to be admitted," Touch the Sky added. "They are both cousins, both of the Panther Clan. Lone Bear will surely accept him now."

Little Horse said something else, but Touch the Sky missed it—he had just spotted Honey Eater, returning from the river with a clay jar full of fresh water.

For a moment he stared at the crude mess Black Elk had left of her hair, so jaggedly cut over her neck it looked as if fire had gnawed away at it. Proudly, defiantly, she had taken no pains to disguise her husband's public mark of shame. Instead of casting her eyes down, as Cheyenne women often did when marked for censure, she boldly met all comers in the eye. Touch the Sky knew she was rebelling against Black Elk's tyranny. He was proud of her spirit, but afraid it would only lead to more trouble for her.

"Black Elk should *receive* the bull whip, not become one," Little Horse said with anger in his voice as he watched Honey Eater cross to her tipi. "Everyone in camp knows he has cut off Honey Eater's braid. Many are angry at this, although some of the warriors say it is Black Elk's business, that it may spoil the hunt to stir up trouble now."

Touch the Sky dropped his glance before Honey Eater could meet it. Not only did he wish to spare her feelings, but he felt that Black Elk was lurking somewhere nearby, watching as usual. Lately, because Black Elk's jealousy had become crazy-dangerous, Touch the Sky went out of his way to avoid chance meetings with or even glances at Honey Eater.

But this only served to charge their occasional accidental meetings with even more meaning. By now it was common knowledge in the clan circles that the two loved each other. The story was told clearly in the way they carefully avoided each other. On occasions when they were forced to be in the same vicinity, they both acted nervous, ill at ease.

One old squaw in the Sky Walker Clan, known as a visionary and a singer, had sung their love in a tragic song. The song did not say their names but was clearly about them. Now all the younger girls were singing it in their sewing lodge. Secretly, they hoped this love would somehow become a marriage.

"Look, buck!" Little Horse nodded across the central camp clearing, toward the hide-covered council lodge.

As if to grimly confirm what they had been talking about, Black Elk, his younger cousin Wolf Who Hunts Smiling, and Lone Bear, head of the Bull Whip soldier society, were conferring together. Now and then one of them glanced across the clearing toward Touch the Sky.

"They are plotting against you," Little Horse said with conviction. "I suspect they have some plan for the Animal Dance this night."

Touch the Sky said nothing, though he feared his friend was right. The Animal Dance was also known as the Crazy Dance or the Buffalo Dance, because it was always given on the night before the tribe left en masse for the hunt. Unlike most of the solemn Cheyenne ceremonies, it was known for its foolish mimicry of animals and sly ridicule of tribe members, which often left many of the observers rolling on the ground in gales of laughter.

Arrow Keeper stepped out from his tipi, which occupied a lone hummock beside Touch the Sky's. He crossed to speak to his apprentice.

"Are you prepared to assist at the dance?" he said.

Touch the Sky nodded. His nervousness was less now that he had successfully assisted the old medicine man at the Spring Dance during the chief-renewal one winter ago. Again Arrow Keeper had carefully rehearsed his part with him.

Now the old shaman too glanced across the clearing toward the trio of braves in front of the council lodge. Like Little Horse, he quickly guessed this signaled new trouble for Touch the Sky.

He pulled his red Hudson's Bay blanket tighter around his shoulders. The lines in his face were deep, like the cracks of a dried-up riverbed. But though the furrow between his eyes was deep in wrinkled folds, the eyes themselves were clear and bright and observed everything.

"Be ready, little brother, for some things we did not practice. I fear your enemies plan to use the dance against you."

Touch the Sky looked at him, waiting for more. But as if he had already said too much, Arrow Keeper changed the subject.

"I have had a medicine dream, and it told me the hunt will go well. Our travois will be heaped with tender hump steaks."

"Then we are fortunate," Little Horse said. "Each year, thanks to the white hunters and their long-killing rifles, we have fewer and fewer herds. Now look how far south we must ride. As young as I am, I recall a time when the buffalo came to us. Now we chase them into enemy lands."

"You speak straight-arrow, Cheyenne," Arrow Keeper said. "More and more white men, even some in the Great Council, are defending the slaughter of the buffalo as the best way to eliminate the red man. And in this thing they are right, for if they take our food and our clothing and our shelters, what is left to live with?"

"Truly," Little Horse said. "I hate the horse-eating Apaches. But in killing the white man's cattle and throat-slashing his ponies, they do right. Only then do the hairy faces know how *we* feel!"

Touch the Sky remained quiet at this, guilt lancing him inside as he recalled his own life among the white men in the river-bend settlement of Bighorn Falls. A buffalo hide was worth about three dollars on the Eastern market. He and his friend Corey Robinson had once laid eager plans to someday make their fortune slaughtering the great shaggy beasts—and never once, in their dream of riches, had they worried about the red man's fate.

Arrow Keeper saw clearly that his young helper was troubled. The old shaman knew full well what had happened to Honey Eater, knew that an innocent girl had been wronged. He also knew how Touch the Sky felt about that girl. The youth had had enough on his mind since Wolf Who Hunts Smiling had spoken against him at council, after the two had returned from the expedition on Wes Munro's keelboat. Cleverly, without actually inventing complete lies, Wolf Who Hunts Smiling had managed to cast suspicion about Touch the Sky's loyalty to the tribe and the Cheyenne Way. Now many still felt he was a white man's dog, not straight-arrow Cheyenne.

For these reasons, Arrow Keeper decided not to mention the rest of his medicine dream.

Yes, the hunt would go well. They would kill and distribute much meat. But in his vision, Arrow Keeper had also seen the four sacred Medicine Arrows which symbolized the fate of his people, and they were drenched in blood.

That night a huge ceremonial fire was lit in the vast square at the center of camp. Everyone attended the Animal Dance except the sentries and the herd guard sent out to protect the ponies grazing farthest from camp.

From the beginning Touch the Sky faced tense moments. Arrow Keeper had surprised his young apprentice by selecting him, before the entire tribe, to be Crooked Pipe Man for the ceremony. This prized role always went to a brave warrior. Many had expected Black Elk to be selected. But in selecting Touch the Sky, Arrow Keeper had reminded the tribe that the youth counted first coup in the critical Tongue River Battle— the great Cheyenne victory against land-grabber Wes Munro and his murderous militiamen.

Black Elk stood close enough, when this announcement came, for Touch the Sky to watch jealous anger spark in his fierce eyes, which were like black agates. In the shifting orange spears of

36

firelight, Touch the Sky stared with grim fascination at the leathery flap where part of Black Elk's ear had been severed by a Bluecoat saber. The warrior had calmly picked up his detached ear, killed the soldier, then later sewn his own ear back on with buckskin thread.

But now Black Elk's anger did not last long. Touch the Sky watched him exchange conspiring glances with Lone Bear, his cousin Wolf Who Hunts Smiling, and Swift Canoe, who like Wolf Who Hunts Smiling had sworn to someday kill Touch the Sky. Black Elk's satisfied grin again reminded Touch the Sky to be prepared.

Though Honey Eater hid it well, Touch the Sky saw pride rise into her face for a moment when Arrow Keeper selected him as Crooked Pipe Man. Her approval heartened Touch the Sky. But truly, he thought with another pang of angry hate toward Black Elk, it is hard for her to face the tribe like this—her hair a ragged clump like a prairie chicken's tail. Yet it could do nothing to mar the flawless amber skin, the beautifully sculpted cheekbones, the slender, shapely body clinging to her buckskin dress.

The Animal Dance was a relaxed entertainment, not a formal ceremony. Touch the Sky wore no ceremonial finery except his mountain-lion skin, a gift from Arrow Keeper blessed with his big medicine. The warriors had left their war bonnets and scalp-laden coup sticks behind. Black Elk wore a fine new leather shirt adorned with beadwork so beautiful that even warriors—who seldom deigned to remark on women's work—openly complimented it.

Touch the Sky knew it was the handiwork of Honey Eater. Her skill was unmatched among Cheyenne women, whose beadwork was easily the finest of all the Plains tribes. Again, despite his vows not to torment himself, Touch the Sky heard the words of his crucial vision at Medicine Lake—the dead Chief Yellow Bear's words, spoken from the Land of Ghosts:

I have seen you bounce your son on your knee, just as I have seen you shed blood for that son and his mother.

But Yellow Bear had not spoken the mother's name. And Honey Eater was married to Black Elk. Why, Touch the Sky rebuked himself as he waited for the signal to take his place, could he not let this thing alone? Why could he not begin to look at other women in the tribe? Certainly, many of them looked at *him*.

All of this just made him miserable. He gave thanks to Maiyun, the Good Supernatural, when Arrow Keeper told the braves who were playing the part of the Four Directions to take their places.

Touch the Sky went to Crooked Pipe Man's place of honor in the dance square, the northeast corner. This was symbolic of the northern lights—a holy place called Where the Food Comes From, the spiritual home of the Big Holy Ones who first taught the Cheyennes their sacred myths and the secret of the Medicine Arrows.

Little Horse had been selected to be Spirit Who Rules the Summer; a brave named Eagle on His Journey was Spirit Who Gives Good Health; and Wolf Who Hunts Smiling was Spirit Who Rules the Ages. As the braves took their places on all four points of the square, Wolf Who Hunts Smiling passed close to Touch the Sky.

The young brave had only eighteen winters behind him, but was already respected as a fierce warrior. He had a wily, cunning face befitting his name and sharp eyes that seemed to dart everywhere at once. Now those eyes mocked his enemy, Touch the Sky, whom he would never forgive for growing up among the hair-face whites who killed Wolf Who Hunts Smiling's father.

The four braves selected to represent the directions danced in tight circles at their stations, knees kicking high as the tribe chanted *"Hi-ya, hi-ya!"*

"Now let the animals talk to us!" shouted Arrow Keeper, the signal for the comic mimicry to begin.

Touch the Sky had wondered why Swift Canoe had disappeared behind the council lodge. Now, as the costumed brave leaped suddenly into the firelight, he realized why.

The tribe burst into a collective roar of laughter as Touch the Sky felt heat creep into his face.

Swift Canoe's hair was greased with kidney fat and stacked on top of his head in the style of the whites. He wore a white man's shirt and trousers and heavy cowhide boots, captured in the Tongue River battle. The boots, especially, drew many stares and shouts of laughter. Clearly he was mocking Touch the Sky's appearance in the early days of his arrival, when he was called White Man's Shoes.

But the most humiliating part of his costume, to Touch the Sky, was the lace shawl he had wrapped about his shoulders. There was no greater insult to a warrior's manhood than to dress him in woman's clothing. To emphasize the point, Swift Canoe made exaggerated shows of emotion with his face—recalling another name, Woman Face, from the days when Touch the Sky had not yet overcome his white man's habit of showing his feelings in his face.

A young brave from the Shield Clan dashed out with a whiskey bottle. It had been filled with dark yarrow tea to resemble the white man's devil water. This brave too wore white man's clothing—a floppy plainsman's hat and a captured Bluecoat blouse, complete with shiny medals. He and Swift Canoe made an exaggerated show of shaking hands, a white man's custom which Indians found hilarious. Again the rest of the tribe burst into wild laughter and shouts of encouragement.

The two then took turns drinking from the bottle. This drew less laughter from the crowd, and more heat into Touch the Sky's face, as the tribe recognized a thinly veiled charge that Touch the Sky was a white man's dog, possibly even a Bluecoat spy.

But the mirth began anew as several young boys burst out from the surrounding trees, hunched under buffalo hides. They played the part of buffalo and charged all around Swift Canoe. He pretended great fear and clumsiness, tripping over the unlaced boots in his drunkenness and ignorance. Swift Canoe was mocking Touch the Sky's mistake, during his warrior training, of getting downwind of the buffalo and ruining hours of work for the hunters by scattering the herd.

The buffalos finally chased Swift Canoe off into the forest, his face twisted in exaggerated fear.

Comanche Raid

The tribe roared its collective appreciation when the capering buffalos returned to the square and performed a scalp dance to celebrate their victory over the white dog. The final touch, which sent even the most straight-faced soldiers of the Bull Whip troop double with mirth, came when the buffalos built a fire and roasted one of the white man's boots, just as a Cheyenne might roast a hump steak.

Honey Eater and Arrow Keeper did not laugh. The cruelty of this drama was not in keeping with the Cheyenne Way, and others besides Little Horse protested by turning their backs. The soldiers would not permit talking during the animal mimicry. Otherwise, Little Horse told himself hotly, he would have remined the troublemaker Swift Canoe that Touch the Sky had saved the tribe more than once to prove he was true Cheyenne.

Touch the Sky now gave his enemies no fuel for more ridicule. His face was alert but impassive, giving not the slightest clue to whatever feelings he held down inside. If his enemies expected him to be broken by this, he thought, they knew little about the courage of blooded warriors.

Black Elk, Lone Bear, and Wolf Who Hunts Smiling all stared at him with mocking eyes, waiting for his anger and humiliation to show.

Arrow Keeper caught his eyes and did something Indians rarely did. He winked at his apprentice.

Touch the Sky was at first confused. Then he understood the subtle hint. Suddenly the blank mask disappeared from his face, replaced by a smile.

The smile broadened, turned to laughter. The laughter bubbled in his chest, grew louder. Touch the Sky doubled over, his body spasming with uncontrollable hilarity.

At first the rest of the tribe was startled. Then their blank expressions turned to amusement and admiration. They too began laughing anew, this time led by their baffling new shaman apprentice. Soon stern warriors rolled on the ground like children, howling at the moon. The whole tribe was involved, led by the tall warrior Touch the Sky's infectious laughter.

The buffalos, totally ignored now, sneaked back into the trees, dragging their hides behind them. Black Elk scowled, embarrassed to have the thunder stolen from his act. He slipped past the soldiers and returned to his tipi, dragging Honey Eater with him.

Arrow Keeper grinned foolishly himself as he watched his young assistant reduce an entire tribe to hysterical giggles. He nodded his approval. It was good that this was happening, that they were laughing. Because soon they not only rode off to a good hunt—they also rode into the teeth of their enemies.

He had seen the blood on the Arrows, and Arrow Keeper knew that laughter, while necessary, always gave way to tears.

Chapter 4

Swift Canoe said, "Congratulations, brother! I see from your pony's tail that you are a Bull Whip now."

Wolf Who Hunts Smiling held his face proudly impassive. The men in his Panther Clan, which included Black Elk, took great pride in showing little concern for the praise of others. But the young brave was fully aware of the new streamers of red and black flannel tied to his pony's tail—the badge of the Bull Whip Society.

All around the two braves, Gray Thunder's people were preparing to move out in a long column behind the hunters. Most of the adults and children old enough to ride were mounted, some using stuffed buffalo-hide saddles, most just blankets. The infants and elderly would ride on travois. Young boys led packhorses tied to lead lines. Black Elk had already sent out flankers to protect the main column on the move. The women, well practiced, were taking down the tipis in minutes. But they would take much longer to erect again.

"What about the initiation?" Swift Canoe said. "When Blue Robe joined the Whips, they tied him up for one entire sleep with a huge rock on his chest."

Wolf Who Hunts Smiling shook his head in scorn. "Lone Bear knew that such children's games were useless in my case. He saw me fight at the Tongue River Battle, saw me kill the first enemy. He said the initiation would not be necessary for a warrior such as I."

Swift Canoe wisely said nothing. But he was thinking that it also didn't hurt that Black Elk was his cousin. Everyone in camp knew by now that Black Elk too had recently tied the Bull Whip streamers to his pony.

"So now you will ride as one of the Hunt Law enforcers," Swift Canoe said, admiration clear in his voice. "Perhaps you can speak for me in one more winter, when I send Lone Bear the gift of arrows?"

"Perhaps," Wolf Who Hunts Smiling said vaguely. Swift Canoe was his fawning imitator and often got on his nerves. He was a capable enough warrior and certainly no coward, though like most in his Wolverine Clan, he was a complainer and often shirked his duties. But he was also a loyal follower, and Wolf Who Hunts Smiling harbored secret plans of ambition, for which he would need loyal followers. For this reason he tolerated Swift Canoe—this, and the fact that

Comanche Raid

Swift Canoe hated Touch the Sky nearly as much as he did, blaming him for the death of his twin brother, True Son.

The two young braves were rigging their ponies for the hunt. Now Swift Canoe said, "Black Elk has blood in his eye over the incident last night. He was sullen with me, as if *I* had anything to do with Touch the Sky's clever victory during the Animal Dance. I played my part well."

"Woman Face will pay dearly for his short moment of glory," Wolf Who Hunts Smiling said. "Black Elk and I are both Hunt Soldiers, and we will be watching him closely. He will taste our whips before the meat is piled on our racks."

Despite Touch the Sky's improved standing among many in the tribe, Wolf Who Hunts Smiling was content. The young brave was as wily as his name. He knew full well that, despite all of Black Elk's courage and skill, he was a child in his feelings. Black Elk used to try to be fair toward the tall newcomer. But his increasing jealousy over Honey Eater had caused him to abandon his usual code of honor.

Once already he had sent Swift Canoe and Wolf Who Hunts Smiling to kill the young buck. They had failed, even after successfully luring a grizzly to his cave at Medicine Lake. But Wolf Who Hunts Smiling felt no shame in this failure—Touch the Sky was a true and mighty warrior. It simply was not possible for Wolf Who Hunts Smiling to achieve his plans if both of them lived.

And judging from the look on Black Elk's sullen face, he thought, Touch the Sky would confront more than the threat of bull whips on this hunt.

*　　*　　*

Once Gray Thunder raised his lance high, signaling the beginning of the hunt, the long column moved out quickly.

It was necessary to move fast because the buffalo moved fast. The great, shaggy beasts always moved at a stampede, stopping only to graze before stampeding on again. The sick, lame, and lazy were forced to the front. Any who stumbled would end up in the bellies of the wolves who worried the fringes of the herds.

Constantly Black Elk kept warriors riding on the flanks. They were in frequent communication with the main body thanks to the efforts of young runners who had been selected because of their swift ponies. Black Elk himself rode point, with the best scouts well out ahead of him. The pace was grueling.

They made good time, but not without mishaps. They were forced to use a bad ford when crossing the Shoshone River. Some tipi covers and poles were lost to the runoff-swollen current. A child nearly drowned when it fell off a pony, but was snatched out of the water by an alert old grandmother.

One sleep into their journey, they passed the awesome Black Hills. The Bowstring and Bull Whip soldiers rode up and down the column, enforcing silence while the sacred center of the Cheyenne world remained in sight.

Touch the Sky marveled again at the Black Hills' beauty. They stretched from the northeastern Wyoming Territory into the Dakota country, a series of rocky, craggy heights rising above the semiarid plain that surrounded them. Lush, dark green forests stood out against barren backgrounds of shale, sandstone, and limestone.

Streams tumbled everywhere.

When the Black Hills were well behind them, and they were approaching the Platte River, Little Horse rode up beside his companion.

"Brother," he said, "I hope you are keeping eyes in the back of your head."

It wasn't necessary to say more—Touch the Sky knew what he meant. Wolf Who Hunts Smiling had made a point of letting him know he was watching him intently. The other Bull Whips too made contemptuous faces when they passed him in the column.

"I am," he replied. "The arrogant Wolf Who Hunts Smiling is waiting to pounce on me at my first mistake. He knows that resisting a hunt soldier is a dangerous business. I cannot even fight back."

"This thing is wrong," Little Horse said. "Arrow Keeper tells me the soldiers were originally limited to making sure no hunter attacked the herds too early once the buffalo were spotted. Now the Bull Whips freely beat anyone at any time during the hunt."

Little Horse looked over his shoulder to make sure a Bull Whip was not riding close.

"Consider the last hunt, what the Whips did to Black Robe of the Root Eaters Clan. He fired on a buffalo before the command was given. The Whips threw him on the ground and beat him until he could not stand. They broke up his weapons. They cut his blankets, moccasins, and kit to shreds. When they had finished, they took all of his food and went off with his horse. They left him alone on the prairie, sore and bleeding, too weak and hurt to move. And the Hunt Law would not permit anyone to help him."

Touch the Sky nodded grimly. "Wolf Who Hunts Smiling has picked a troop to his liking."

"Truly, brother. Hold that thought close to your heart, especially after making a fool of Black Elk and Swift Canoe at the Animal Dance. They are *for* you, buck!"

The Kiowa scout named Stone Mountain peered out past the rimrock, watching the long Cheyenne column advance below on the plain.

He and his Comanche companion, Kicking Bird, had been camped for many sleeps here in the steep hills just north of the Smoky Hill River, well south of the Wyoming-Colorado border. Stone Mountain was aptly named. The huge Kiowa was even taller than his leader, Hairy Wolf, and his shoulders were so massive he had been forced to cut a slit across the back of his captured Bluecoat blouse in order to put it on. His thick black hair fell past the base of his spine.

"*Maldita sea*," Kicking Bird cursed in Spanish. "Now we must finally leave this fine camp."

Stone Mountain nodded glumly. He had been glad to leave the hot, dry ravines and canyons and arroyos of the Staked Plain behind them. They had found this place and used it as a base camp when spying on the Cheyenne's advance scouts. But now the tribe had finally reached this far south, and he and Kicking Bird would have to give up this safe, snug place with its good hunting and clear, cold water. It was time to head back now and alert the main band.

True, there were far more blue-dressed soldiers

up north. But the two Indians were so used to finding cover in the desert that they could move with ease up here. Even when trees were scarce, one could hunker down in the waist-tall buffalo grass.

Stone Mountain left a little leather pouch with a few beads inside under a rock in the center of the camp—it was the Kiowa way to leave a gift to a place that had been good to them.

"Watching the Cheyenne tribe on the move is a child's job," Kicking Bird said. "But I would rather sneak into a bear's den than spy on their camps. Their dogs are many and raise a clamor at the first smell of an enemy."

Stone Mountain nodded. Dogs were also likely to make a racket at the wrong time. For this reason the Cheyennes left them behind when riding into battle or the hunt.

"It was the Cheyenne," he said, "fighting beside their cousins the Sioux and their allies the Arapaho who first drove the Kiowa out of this fine land. At one time we shared the Kansas and Nebraska ranges with the Pawnee. This green land is our rightful homeland. Now look how they fly right into our faces again! Will they not be content until we are camped in Sonora?"

The two scouts had moved down below the rimrock to untether their ponies. Kicking Bird, who craved tobacco badly, paused to split his wooden pipe open with a rock. Eagerly, he sucked at the brown gum inside it.

"Take heart, brother," Stone Mountain said as he swung his huge bulk onto the back of his sturdy buckskin pony. "You saw the women and children just now. Prices are good in Santa Fe.

49

There will be no shortage of fine tobacco if this raid goes as planned!"

Three sleeps into the hunt journey, Gray Thunder's Cheyennes sighted the Arkansas River. The largest and most treacherous of all the rivers on the Southern Plains, it wound from the Colorado Rockies across the Plains to the huge river the Indians called Great Waters, the whites the Mississippi.

Fresh meat was needed for the trail. One of the braves who had lived in this area with the Southern Cheyennes recalled that a huge salt lick, which attracted game, was located nearby. Gray Thunder called for volunteers to search for it.

Touch the Sky and Little Horse were among the braves who rode off from the main column. They all fanned out, dividing the river valley into sections for the search. Touch the Sky nudged his gray toward a stretch of thickets just past a huge bend in the river.

The salt licks were places where earth surrounded saline springs. The vast amount of salt which accumulated brought deer, elk, and antelope in fantastic numbers. Touch the Sky tethered his pony and entered the thickets on foot, searching for fresh game prints.

He searched the river bank in both directions, finding signs only of rabbits and other small game. He had returned to his pony, and was about to break out of the thickets onto the plain when, suddenly, he felt a sharp tug at his legging sash.

A sapling behind him suddenly split; a heartbeat later, the sharp crack of a rifle reached his ears. Only then did Touch the Sky realize that the tug was a bullet which had reached him before the sound of the rifle—he was being fired upon!

Instinctively, he leaped out of the line of fire. But he couldn't retreat deeper into the thickets while his pony was tethered in the open.

He leaped out of the thickets and raced toward his horse. But when he glanced out across the short-grass expanse, he spotted no enemies closing in—only Black Elk accompanied by two other riders. Touch the Sky waited for them to reach him.

"Do not stand there gaping as if you were beholding the Wendigo, mooncalf!" Black Elk said as he dismounted. He was accompanied by Tangle Hair, the Bowstring Soldier who had settled the dispute over Honey Eater's braid, and Lone Bear, the leader of the Bull Whip soldiers. "A wounded elk may be escaping. I shot at one just now. Help us find it."

"You have found your elk already," Touch the Sky said.

He grabbed his buckskin legging sash and twisted it until they could see the small hole where Black Elk's bullet had torn through.

Black Elk's face revealed nothing. There was silence for several heartbeats while Lone Bear exchanged a long glance with his troop's newest warrior. Touch the Sky watched both men carefully.

"Truly," Black Elk said, "from where I stood, I was shooting at an elk."

"It is common at such distances," Lone Bear said, "to mistake buckskin clothing for an elk's hide. Indeed, palefaces are always shooting each other this way. Do I speak straight-arrow, Tangle Hair?"

Tangle Hair was young, only a soldier and not head of a troop as Lone Bear was. Besides, why did this tall Cheyenne always manage to be in the middle of trouble? Nonetheless, Tangle Hair could not help admiring him. He was no brave to fool with. Besides, Tangle Hair had been patrolling the flanks of the column when Touch the Sky entered that thicket—and he could have sworn Black Elk too had seen him enter.

"You speak straight-arrow indeed," Tangle Hair finally replied. "It is a common mistake. Good thing for Touch the Sky that Black Elk's aim was not a cat's whisker better."

"Yes," Black Elk said, staring at Touch the Sky with the hint of a smile playing at his lips. "Good thing."

Chapter 5

Two sleeps passed after the incident in the thicket. Touch the Sky kept a wary eye on his enemies while the land all around him gradually changed as the tribe pushed further south, following the buffalo trail.

There was still enough grass, especially near the rivers, to support the buffalo herds. But more and more now Touch the Sky noticed flowering mescal, the white plumes of the tall, narrow cactus known as Spanish Bayonet, and the low-hanging pods of mesquite. Now they had to be careful to keep the horses and children from drinking bad alkali water.

Touch the Sky was riding by himself on flank guard when Spotted Tail, leader of the Bowstrings, rode out from the main column to join him.

"I would speak with you," Spotted Tail said, his pony falling into step beside Touch the Sky's. The brave had 30 winters behind him. But the white streaks in the back of his hair, which had earned him his name, had appeared in his youth.

"I always have ears for words spoken by the leader of the Bowstrings," Touch the Sky said with genuine respect.

"This is a delicate matter." Spotted Tail glanced out across the mesquite-pocked range, toward the main body. Touch the Sky knew he was watching for Bull Whip soldiers.

"I saw you count first coup at the Tongue River Battle," said Spotted Tail. "I have watched you since you arrived at our camp. I have heard the charges against you. Indeed, I was among those who voted for your execution when you were first charged as a spy for the blue blouses. I am glad now that old Arrow Keeper intervened to save you. After watching you fight at Tongue River, I will never question your loyalty to Gray Thunder's tribe. You are a warrior, buck, and straight-arrow Cheyenne all the way through!"

These were important words, coming from the leader of the tribe's most popular soldier society. But Touch the Sky held his face impassive, as warriors did. A man who knew he had earned praise never showed gratitude for it.

"However, many in the tribe—many in my own society—disagree with me. Some think that a Cheyenne who once wore white man's shoes and lived under a roof can never be a Cheyenne. For this reason I cannot follow my heart and invite you to undergo the initiation into the Bowstrings—not yet."

Touch the Sky nodded, understanding this thing. No Indian leader, be he a chief, a clan headman, or a military society leader, could dictate to his followers.

"However," said Spotted Tail, glancing again toward the main column, "that is not why I rode out here. I came to tell you that you better play the sharp-eyed hawk during this journey. Something is afoot with the Bull Whips. They have plans for you. In this they are spurred on by Black Elk and his hotheaded young cousin. Indeed, it was to make your life miserable, I believe, that Black Elk left the Bowstrings."

Touch the Sky nodded. "There was a time when he felt nothing but cold contempt for me. Now he hates me."

"Everyone knows why," Spotted Tail said, not bothering to elaborate. "Know this. I have told my Bowstrings, watch not only the people, but the Whips too. They are no men to fool with. Nor are many of them honorable—more than one has stolen meat from Bowstring racks.

"But though I have asked my troop to watch over you, some will refuse to help. Those who are opposed to you say it does not matter that you are brave and strong. They say you are still a lone coyote without a clan and therefore loyal only to yourself. So be wary like a fox. Do not give the Bull Whips the smallest reason for noticing you."

Touch the Sky nodded, thanking the warrior before Spotted Tail rode back to join the main column. His words left the tall brave apprehensive, but determined. He had sworn this thing

55

to his friend Little Horse when Touch the Sky returned from Medicine Lake after his vision: He was home to stay. Anyone who planned to drive him out now would have to either kill him or die in the attempt.

As if to reassure himself, his hand dropped to the butt-plate of the percussion-action Sharps protruding from his scabbard. The weapon had been a gift from his white father in Bighorn Falls. But if the soldiers chose to invoke the strict Hunt Law, as an excuse for "punishing" him, he would not be free to fight back.

Despite these worries, the increasing excitement of the tribe, as they drew nearer to the buffalo, infected Touch the Sky too. Several of the hunters carried their specially blessed buffalo shields, depicting the tufted tails and woolly humps of the great shaggy creatures. In camp at night, the children who'd been on previous hunts lorded it over the younger ones and kept repeating, "Wait until you *see* them!" The braves said little. They smiled and looked away, embarrassed to admit that they too were affected by the excitement—though obviously they were.

They were fully aware that this mesa and ravine country was the home of their enemies, the Kiowa and Comanche. The far-flung flankers and scouts sent back word of any movements by red men or blue-bloused soldiers. Black Elk, reckless in battle, showed great prudence when responsible for the entire tribe—at the least sign of potential danger, he led the column wide around it. As was Cheyenne custom, they rode under a white truce flag to announce this was not a hostile movement.

Comanche Raid

They reached a series of sandstone rises between the Canadian River and the Red River. The spot offered plenty of water, good protection from the sand-laden winds, and plenty of drift cottonwood to make excellent fires. Black Elk called a halt for the day, giving the order to make camp.

Touch the Sky and Little Horse were ordered to backtrack some distance and make a "false camp." This consisted of building a few fires and leaving a few ponies tethered in the area. It would serve as a decoy. If attacked by Kiowa or Comanche, the racket would alert the real camp upriver.

By the time they returned to the main camp, Touch the Sky was famished. Little Horse joined his clan circle, and Touch the Sky crossed to Arrow Keeper's fire. As usual, the old shaman had cooked meat for him too, and prepared extra yarrow tea.

While he ate, Touch the Sky saw Honey Eater crossing to join the women of her clan. After the hunt, the hunters would congregate for hours and boast about their kills. But the hard work of skinning and butchering would fall to the women and children.

Touch the Sky carefully avoided looking at her. Black Elk's jealousy had softened the warrior's brain, and Touch the Sky knew he was on the feather-edge of killing both him and Honey Eater. He would do nothing to set the hot-tempered warrior off.

On the other hand, he was determined to keep as close an eye on Honey Eater as he possibly could. The murder stigma was strong, but Touch the Sky would sully the Arrows if necessary to

57

protect the woman he loved with all his heart.

Arrow Keeper glanced at the youth's face and read some of these conflicting thoughts in the flickering firelight as they ate.

"Will you be riding herd guard again, little brother?" the shaman asked him.

Touch the Sky nodded. He had learned a valuable lesson from the hunt journey: When the tribe stopped for the day, always send the ponies out farther away from camp during the early part of the evening, under guard. That way they could graze until moved in closer during the late hours, yet there would still be grass left for them near camp.

"The duty is unpopular," Touch the Sky said. "But I volunteer because of your advice that a shaman should seek time alone. And truly, Father, I have come to enjoy the time spent with the ponies."

"This is a good thing. A shaman, like a chief, must love and serve his people. But he is not as afraid as most to spend time alone, meditating and observing. Only by listening closely to the language of Nature can you learn her secrets. Still . . ."

Arrow Keeper gazed beyond the circle of the fire, past Touch the Sky and off into the grainy twilight of the Southwestern Plains.

He was thinking of his medicine dream, his vision of blood staining the sacred arrows. And he was thinking of this feeling now, this premonition which stained the air. This was enemy territory, after all.

"Still," he repeated, "shaman or no, it is also a good thing to keep your weapons at hand."

Comanche Raid

* * *

Touch the Sky's gray was exhausted, so he let her rest. Instead, he cut a good little paint out of the herd and rode north of camp, toward the Red River, to guard the ponies grazing the bunchgrass farther out. Wolf Who Hunts Smiling and several other Bull Whips watched him closely. But Arrow Keeper too was watching, and they left him alone.

The sun had bled slowly out of the western sky, leaving a blue-black dome smattered with glittering stars. Spanish Bayonets rose tall and dark against the skyline. Now and then coyotes barked—a series of fast yelps ending in a long howl that made Touch the Sky's hackles rise.

The portion of the herd he was protecting was grazing close to the river. Touch the Sky gave the paint her head and let her wander and graze, only occasionally nudging her into movement to bunch the ponies a little tighter.

Finally they settled in one area. He dismounted and took up a position with his back against a cottonwood, his Sharps lying across his legs. From here he commanded a view of the long, moonlit rise which was the best line of attack.

Despite his vigilance, Touch the Sky was weary. He had been up with the sun, ridden guard on the flanks, then doubled back with Little Horse to set up the false camp. Now he would remain with the ponies until they were called in for the night.

For a time, despite his determination to the contrary, his mind was filled with thoughts and images of Honey Eater. But slowly, as his weary muscles began to grow slack, he pushed

59

the thoughts aside and listened to nothing but the bubbling chuckle of the river, the eerie rhythm of cicadas, the occasional nickering or snorting or stamping of the horses.

Then, even those noises blended together, then faded. His eyes appeared glazed over, he sat absolutely motionless, and even his breathing seemed suspended.

Once again Touch the Sky saw images from his powerful vision at Medicine Lake, only they flew past like rapid birds and he glimpsed them only for a heartbeat. But when the words were spoken clearly inside his head, it was not the voices of the dead who had spoken in his vision—it was Arrow Keeper's:

Wake to the living world now, little brother, or sing your death song!

An instant later Touch the Sky blinked, and he stared into the war paint of a Comanche!

From the vivid descriptions given by Arrow Keeper and others, he knew immediately it was a Comanche, despite never having seen one close up. A large, cruel mouth was made even more ferocious with streaks of their brilliant green and yellow war paint. His ears were pierced with large brass hoops, and a bear-claw necklace dangled around his neck. His small but lethal skull-cracker was raised at the ready. Two more steps closer, and he would have dashed Touch the Sky's brains out against the tree.

Touch the Sky raised his rifle off his lap and slid his finger inside the trigger guard.

But when he aimed out into the darkness, the Comanche was gone.

Comanche Raid

For a long moment the dumbfounded Cheyenne simply sat there, stupidly aiming at nothing. Slowly, the muzzle of his rifle lowered, and he asked himself: Had the Comanche brave disappeared like a thing of smoke because he *was* a thing of smoke? A fancy coined by Touch the Sky's tired, overwrought brain?

But no! He had been so real Touch the Sky could count the quills in his moccasins. Their enemy was upon them!

Quickly he slipped the paint's hackamore back on, then rounded up the ponies and pointed them toward the main camp. It was nearly time to drive them in anyway, as he could see from the position of the Always Star to the north.

Touch the Sky had been filled with his news as he rounded up the ponies. And he had kept a sharp lookout for more Comanches. But now, as he added these ponies to the herd near camp, doubts again assailed him. True, the Comanches were famous for stealth. But how could *any* Indian simply be there one instant, gone the next?

By the time Touch the Sky returned to camp, few people were interested in his news. Scouts had just returned with news that the buffalo birds had been spotted! These were the parasites that traveled with the buffalo, living off the ticks in their hide. Whenever they were discovered, the herd was close by. Now the camp was buzzing with talk and preparations.

"Tomorrow, brother, we eat hot livers!" Little Horse greeted him triumphantly. "I will kill a huge bull and tie its beard to my pony's tail!"

Touch the Sky took his news to Spotted Tail of the Bowstrings. He listened closely. Then he said, "Black Elk has taken too many precautions, there could not be a large war party nearby. It was only a lone renegade, hoping to steal ponies. You scared him off."

Arrow Keeper said little when he told him the story. He only stared long into the fire, his eyes dark, glittering chips of obsidian. After a time, Touch the Sky thought he had fallen asleep. The old medicine man nodded off more and more now, seemed to tire more easily.

But he suddenly reached out and stirred the fire with a green stick. A column of sparks flew up with the smoke. Outside the warmth of the clan fires, another coyote howled.

"It hardly matters, little brother, whether the warrior you saw was real or not. Either way, you saw him. It is a warning. Gray Thunder's tribe is marked for grave danger."

Chapter 6

"Soon they will attack the herd," Hairy Wolf said. "So we must strike soon too."

He and the Comanche leader Iron Eyes sat their ponies where they had stopped their bands at a water hole in the Texas Panhandle. They were still south of the Cheyenne tribe. The land hereabouts was cracked and dried from the sere summer heat. The grass was thin and brittle, and the midday sunshine drew heavy sweat that mixed with the dust coating every Indian, forming a paste.

Their combined bands had ridden north from the Blanco Canyon camp after receiving favorable reports from the scouts Stone Mountain and Kicking Bird.

"Remember," said Iron Eyes, leader of the Quohada Comanches, "we must stay out of sight of the hunters. There are too many warriors for us to take on, especially now that they are keen for the hunt blood."

Iron Eyes truly respected the Cheyenne as warriors. But what kind of men permitted themselves only one wife? He himself currently had three, and if any one of them crossed him, he would simply kill her and take another as Comanche law allowed. Women were like horses, there were more to be had.

"Yes," Hairy Wolf agreed. "Our target is the hunt camp itself. It will be under light guard unless we are spotted."

The giant Kiowa leader was bigger than every member of his band except Stone Mountain. His rich black mane of hair flew out behind him now as a dust-laden wind kicked up. He was dressed in captured cavalry trousers and high-topped riding boots, and was bare from the waist up except for his sturdy bone breastplate.

"We hit fast," Iron Eyes said. "We lash the prisoners to the spare ponies; then we count on the superior speed of our horses to stay ahead of the Cheyenne if they come for us. They will never touch us in the Blanco."

Behind the two leaders, Painted Lips and some of the others towed extra mounts on lead lines. Big Tree, the Comanche who could shoot 20 arrows while an enemy fired and reloaded a rifle twice, had painted his face in vertical and horizontal stripes of black, the color of death.

"No," agreed Hairy Wolf, "once in the canyon the fight is ours to win. When it is safe, we will then mount an expedition to Santa Fe to meet the Comancheros. We will take no fat or ugly or

old women, nor children still sucking at the dug—
these are hard to sell."

"Straight words, Kaitsenko. And these are Cheyennes, so we must remember to get the knives
which all the young girls wear around their necks.
They will kill themselves if we do not."

"Then they are more vigilant than their savage lords," Hairy Wolf said scornfully. "Dog Fat
claims he nearly walked up to a herd guard and
brained him against a tree where he sat dream-
ing."

But despite these brave words, both leaders
respected and feared the Cheyenne. This was
clear as they set out again. Iron Eyes turned and
started the word with Painted Lips: *Remember
Wolf Creek!*

The rallying cry spread quickly through the
ranks as the two bands moved north.

Early the next morning the hunters rode out.
The buffalo birds had been spotted near enough
by then that the Cheyenne decided against moving the hunt camp. It was necessary to keep the
women and children close by for the skinning and
butchering should the kill go well.

Black Elk naturally assumed that enemy scouts
were in the area. But the reports from his own
scouts strongly confirmed his own sense that no
large deployment of warriors was in the vicinity.
The hunt would be near enough to the camp,
which would be safe under the protection of a
few junior warriors-in-training.

Touch the Sky's strong feelings of anticipation
affected his pony. It wanted to run, but he held
her in. The hunters kept their horses to a walk,

65

planning to unleash them only at the last moment, when the buffalo had sensed them and started their inevitable stampede.

These were the critical moments of the hunt, and the soldier societies were in full force. Despite the Cheyenne brave's respect for custom and the tribal law-ways, they were a warrior society—the traits needed in a good warrior were not always in harmony with those of a good tribe member. The rash, reckless, fearless bravery of individual effort was what decided Indian battles. The honor of counting first coup went to the warrior who moved first, acting on his own.

This strong tradition of individual effort meant that the hunters naturally got carried away in the competition to kill the first buffalo, a high honor indeed. But a herd warned too early could escape, and thus an entire people go hungry and poorly clothed because of one man's rashness. So the Bowstrings and the Bull Whips rode on either flank. They would not leave their vigilant guard positions, and join the hunt, until the hunt leader signaled the charge.

River of Winds had been selected as hunt leader. Talking would be permitted, in low voices, until he gave the command for silence. Little Horse nudged his pony up beside his friend.

"Brother," he said, "I have been thinking about Black Elk's shot into the thickets. Ride close to me during the hunt so no more 'accidents' like this happen."

Touch the Sky nodded, his lips pressed into their determined slit as he glanced to both sides of the wedge-shaped formation. Black Elk rode slightly ahead of him. Wolf Who Hunts Smiling rode directly across from him on the flank, in line with the other Bull Whips. Certainly another accident could happen easily.

"Once the hunt is underway," Touch the Sky said, "we will move well away from the others."

Further conversation ceased as River of Winds signaled the command for silence. They were approaching the last long rise before the spot where the scouts had last spotted the herd. And Touch the Sky could see the tiny buffalo birds flitting about, sure proof the buffalo were near.

The wind was favorable for the hunters, blowing hard into their faces. Buffalo were nearly blind, but possessed an extraordinary sense of smell. Touch the Sky could not help thinking about Swift Canoe's Animal Dance antics, heat rising into his face. Once before he had carelessly frightened off the herd by getting downwind of them.

But former disasters faded from his mind as he cautiously walked his horse up to the crest of the last rise overlooking the herd. He joined the long line of waiting hunters, getting his first glimpse of the beasts.

The sight made belly flies stir in his stomach.

The herd was grazing in a lush valley, bright with thick patches of golden crocuses growing against the deep green of the grass. From the rim of the canyon walls rising above them, giant stands of cactus stood like timeless sentinels.

Touch the Sky couldn't even estimate how many there were—so many they formed a great, shaggy carpet that seemed to cover the land as far as the eye could see, heaving and rolling like a giant wave.

More luck was with the hunters. Just past the neck of the valley, the herd's only escape route, was a series of steep-sided sand dunes. When the buffalo were chased into these, their hooves would flounder helplessly.

So far the men had escaped notice. Several ponies wanted to surge forward and were barely restrained by their riders. The desire to draw first hunt blood filled each Cheyenne and made his blood sing. When River of Winds finally dropped his streamered lance, and the line of hunters surged forward, their collective shout rose above the thundering of their ponies' hooves.

As they had agreed, Touch the Sky and Little Horse angled off from the other hunt groups, avoiding the Whips. Their ponies raced down the slope into the thick of the herd, which was only now coming to life as the dominant bulls bellowed the stampede call.

One moment Touch the Sky saw green grass racing below his feet; the next he was swept up in the stampede, and nothing was visible all around him but shaggy brown fur and dangerously sharp horns. The air was clamorous with the sound of hooves pounding, calves bawling, cows lowing, bulls roaring their angry roar. Sometimes the buffalo pressed in so tight his legs were trapped between them and his pony.

Bulls constantly tried to gore his pony. But the gray was too quick, nimbly lunging to safety each time. He saw Little Horse flashing in and out of the swirling dust, bouncing wildly on top his pony. Touch the Sky's Sharps was loaded and ready in his hand. But he knew it was suicide to simply shoot at a buffalo in the main part of a stampede like this—as it went down it could cause a choke-point, throwing the hunter to sure death by trampling.

It was the Cheyenne way to hunt buffalo by skillfully moving to isolate one portion of the vast herd. Then, turning it from the main body, they would close in on it tighter and tighter—much as they fought the white man's circular defense for wagons, attacking in an ever-tightening pattern.

Within a short time he and Little Horse had bunched a group off to the right of the main herd. They were adeptly pointing the stampeding animals toward the sand dunes, whistling, shouting their war cry. Abruptly, several of the biggest bulls veered sharply away from the buffalo they were pointing. Touch the Sky didn't even need to rein the gray—she leaped after the buffalos with a mind of her own.

A few heartbeats later, Touch the Sky's eyes widened in shock when the buffalos suddenly disappeared!

He realized why just in time to rein in his pony before she too plunged over the blind cliff which had just sent the buffalo to their death.

He turned to look behind him. Little Horse, intent on driving their bunch into the dunes, had missed all this. But someone else had seen it. And now, as he raced over to join Touch the Sky, the tall young brave stared with dread at the red and black streamers tied to his pony's tail.

"Woman Face!" Wolf Who Hunts Smiling shouted above the din of the hunt, receding now behind them. "Surrender your weapons! I command this in the name of the Hunt Soldiers!"

"Why?" the warrior demanded. "I have done nothing to violate the Hunt Law."

"Done nothing?" Wolf Who Hunts Smiling nodded behind him, in the direction of the cliff. "Hunting by yourself, you sent at least a dozen fine bulls over a cliff. The Hunt Law strictly forbids solitary kills—no hunter rode anywhere near you! Now these animals are contaminated and cannot be touched."

"I did not chase them over the cliff. They escaped in that direction. I did not know about the cliff until they went over."

"So you say. I saw it differently. Save it for my leader, Lone Bear. I said surrender your weapons!"

Wolf Who Hunts Smiling held his Colt rifle, which had belonged to Touch the Sky in the days when he was still called Matthew Hanchon, aimed at the brave. Reluctantly, Touch the Sky obeyed. As much as he despised Wolf Who Hunts Smiling, disobeying a Hunt Soldier was a serious offense.

His enemy's wily face was triumphant. The swift, furtive eyes mocked him. Clearly, this moment made up for the brief moment of glory when Touch the Sky had ruined Swift Canoe's Animal Dance mimicry.

"You have done it now, *shaman* who likes to laugh at his own unmanly mistakes! We shall see if the others laugh with you and roll upon the ground *now*!"

Wolf Who Hunts Smiling cracked his new, knotted-thong whip hard.

"You'll soon taste this. We'll see then how much laughing Woman Face does!"

70

Chapter 7

Soon the buffalo had thundered on toward the mountain peaks to the west, yellow-brown dust clouds boiling up behind them.

The kill had gone well and the hunters were exhilarated. They had already made the first cut of the butchering, to reach inside and dig out the still-warm livers. They ate them raw from their cupped hands, savoring the hot, tender mouthfuls.

At first they were busy exchanging excited comments about the hunt and the delicious hump steaks they would feast on later. They were slow to notice that the new Bull Whip soldier, Wolf Who Hunts Smiling, held Touch the Sky prisoner. Curiosity took over once they saw something was afoot—quickly they gathered around the pair.

Little Horse was less curious. He knew full well that his friend's enemies had managed to stir up some new trouble. The timing could not be worse for Touch the Sky. Arrow Keeper had ridden out to observe the hunt, as had Chief Gray Thunder. But by law the chief could not hunt, and Arrow Keeper had joked that he no longer had any desire to die anywhere but in his sleep. They had ridden back, after tasting warm liver with the hunters, to supervise the moving of camp. The rest of the tribe must be brought up to butcher the first day's kill.

That meant, Little Horse thought grimly as he joined the others, that by the Hunt Law a soldier troop's decision was final. Worse, the two military societies were independent of each other. Each must respect the other's decisions. And *this* was now a Bull Whip matter.

"What is the meaning of this?" Lone Bear demanded.

"This one," Wolf Who Hunts Smiling said, "deliberately hunted by himself and used a buffalo jump to kill many bulls! Look, below lies the proof!"

"He lives up to his name," Touch the Sky said, "by speaking in a wolf bark. I never saw this cliff. I was chasing buffalo that strayed from the group which Little Horse and I were driving toward the dunes."

"He speaks the straight word," Little Horse said. "We were hunting together. Nor did I see this cliff. Look here how it—"

"Silence!" Lone Bear commanded. "You jabber on like a squaw."

Comanche Raid

Touch the Sky's glance shifted from Wolf Who Hunts Smiling to Swift Canoe to Black Elk. All were gloating, enjoying it immensely as they anticipated the outcome. As if he couldn't hold off, Wolf Who Hunts Smiling kept flicking his whip.

Lone Bear stared at Touch the Sky where he stood beside his pony. "The Hunt Law is strict on the number of buffalo a tribe may kill. This is because Maiyun has ordered that we may take from this earth only what we require to live. Thus the buffalo jump may be used only when there are no horses for the chase, no weapons for the kill. Entire herds have gone over cliffs, dying and rotting in numbers too great to imagine. *You* could have caused it again today."

Touch the Sky tried to speak up, but Swift Canoe was first.

"This is our greatest complaint against the hair faces. We take only what is needed; *they* waste all they can. And here before us stands one of them."

"You swell up with righteousness," Touch the Sky said. "Why not also tell them, *noble warrior,* how you hid like a white-livered coward and tried to murder me at Medicine Lake, sullying our tribe's Sacred Arrows."

"This is not Medicine Lake," Lone Bear said, "and Swift Canoe has not been arrested by one of my soldiers—*you* have, buck! I have ears for Swift Canoe's words. *This*"—Lone Bear pointed over the cliff—"is just one more proof that you have little respect for the Cheyenne Way."

The rest of the hunters exchanged troubled, embarrassed glances. The hunt celebration had been on their minds until this. Only a few times in their memories had the hunt soldiers been forced to discipline a brave for a violation this serious. This Touch the Sky, he was a straight enough warrior. But how did he always manage to be where trouble was?

"Brothers!" Black Elk called out. "This could ruin the rest of the hunt! Our kill today was good, but we need much more meat for the cold moons. His presence may have put the stink upon us so the herds will smell us every time."

"This trail is taking a wrong turn," Little Horse said. "Lone Bear says I jabber on like a woman, but have I not slain our enemies and counted coup like a man? When did Little Horse ever hide behind a better fighter? I say Touch the Sky speaks straight-arrow. He did *not* chase the buffalo over the cliff. They led him toward it."

"True it is that Little Horse can fight. But everyone knows," Wolf Who Hunts Smiling said scornfully, "that he is quick to play the dog for this white man wrapped in a Cheyenne skin. My cousin Black Elk, our war leader, is right. The stink is on him, he will scatter the herds!"

The blood of Wolf Who Hunts Smiling was up now. He harbored great ambitions for tribal leadership. The others were listening respectfully to his words, which lent them a fiery eloquence.

"Red brothers! Only think on this thing. Brother Buffalo knows it is the white men who are exterminating him, not the Indian. And *this* make-believe Cheyenne carries the white smell on him.

"Brothers, have you never caught a skunk's spray direct on your clout or leggings? It *never* washes out. The same with the white man's stink. Black Elk has taught this one the warrior ways, and he does not lack courage. But he is a white man at heart, and his face will soon show his feelings for all to see."

As he finished speaking he cracked his knotted rawhide whip to emphasize his point. This oration stirred several others to approving nods.

"You puff yourself up like the white fools who jump on stumps to speak," Touch the Sky said defiantly. "Like their lies, yours are worth no more than a pig's afterbirth."

Wolf Who Hunts Smiling's sneer twisted into a snarl of rage. He raised his whip to strike, but Little Horse deftly swung his lance out to stop it. The gesture was useless, however, because Lone Bear now spoke up again.

"Enough of this quarreling! Are we women in their sewing lodge? The Hunt Law is clear on these matters. Now the whips will speak with much sharper tongues."

Lone Bear nodded once. The Bull Whips prepared to set upon Touch the Sky.

"Warriors! Hear my words!"

The speaker was Spotted Tail, leader of the Bowstrings.

"In the Bowstrings we require more proof than the word of one witness, an enemy of the accused man at that. Recall, Wolf Who Hunts Smiling now speaks against Touch the Sky after openly walking between him and the camp fire! Do we trust a witness who has thus threatened to kill the very buck he now accuses?"

Black Elk, sparks snapping in his fierce dark eyes, whirled toward the Bowstring leader.

Judd Cole

"You have called my cousin a liar. Very well. Do you also call me a liar?"

Spotted Tail bit back his words. He was no coward, but Black Elk was certainly no warrior to provoke when he was keen for a fight as he clearly was now. Getting killed, Spotted Tail told himself, would not help Touch the Sky.

Thus seeing which way the wind must set for now, Spotted Tail called out, "Bowstrings! If you honor justice, turn your ponies!"

As one, the soldiers of the Bowstring troop joined their leader in turning their ponies around. By turning their backs, they protested the Bull Whip's actions; by remaining, they supported Cheyenne law. Several other hunters belonging to neither of the troops also joined the Bowstrings in turning their backs.

Touch the Sky refused to flinch back when the Bull Whips advanced upon him, Black Elk and Wolf Who Hunts Smiling riding at the head of the pack behind Lone Bear. It was the usual custom for the troop leader to strike the first blow. But now Lone Bear nudged his pony to one side, letting the other two advance first.

Black Elk and his younger cousin exchanged a quick glance. Wolf Who Hunts Smiling nodded slightly, also dropping back. Black Elk rode forward, turned his pony, and raised his whip. His hate-glazed eyes met Touch the Sky's, and his words proved it was Honey Eater on his mind, not violations of Hunt Law.

"You squaw-stealing dog," he said in a voice meant just for Touch the Sky's ears. "Your hot blood will cool once it drips into the Plains!"

The corded muscles of his shoulders bunched tightly as he lashed out savagely with the knotted rawhide, expertly cracking it across Touch the Sky's chest and ripping open a burning line of flesh. The incredible pain jolted Touch the Sky, but though he winced he refused to cry out or show the pain in his face.

Again and again Black Elk brought his whip down, ripping, tearing, opening up lacerations all over Touch the Sky's body. Only when Black Elk's arm began to tire did the rest set upon him.

Now, despite all his efforts, Touch the Sky was driven to his knees by the sheer force of the pain. Little Horse made as if to leap from his pony, but the braves on either side restrained him.

The whips hissed and cracked, and Touch the Sky's blood flowed in scarlet ribbons into the ground. Every nerve ending in his body seemed to have been stripped raw and held up to a flame. But though he was on the ground now, he refused to cry out or show anything but defiance in his face.

"Cry, Woman Face!" Wolf Who Hunts Smiling taunted him, breathing heavily from his exertions with the whip. "Twist up your face like the newborns do and make your chin quiver!"

A moment later Wolf Who Hunts Smiling leaped back in rage when Touch the Sky hawked up a wad of phlegm and spat it into his face. This made Wolf Who Hunts Smiling strike even harder, but Touch the Sky still refused to cry out— even though now he was so bloody the soil clung to him like brown bark.

In a fury of sudden strength, Little Horse broke free of the braves restraining him and leaped from his pony. Screaming the war cry, he waded among the flailing whips, catching them, tangling them, jerking one from its owner's hand, taking the lashes meant for his friend. One hand flew to his beaded sheath and removed his knife.

"Hold! The first Bull Whip who comes close enough dies a hard death!"

The Bull Whip soldiers stopped, looking to Lone Bear for their instructions. Lone Bear considered carefully. He knew that his troop was not eager to flog Little Horse—a brave honored in council for his fighting courage when he had only 15 winters behind him. Yet the leader of the Bull Whips was no man to trifle with.

"Black Elk!" he called out. "What do you counsel?"

Black Elk's blood was still up from the beating. Now his nostrils flared wide with his hard breathing.

"Little Horse is too much influenced by Touch the Sky. But he is a warrior unlikely to die in his sleep."

"I have seen him fight like five men," another Bull Whip said.

"Brothers! These things are straight enough," Wolf Who Hunts Smiling said. "But only think on this! He plays the dog for one who openly drinks strong water with the hair faces, one who leaves messages in the forks of trees for Bluecoat soldier chiefs. *I* have not forgotten the sight when Bluecoat canister shot butchered my father as surely as our women will soon butcher these buffalo! Now Little Horse has brazenly defied Cheyenne law by interfering with a soldier troop! Whip him too!"

Lone Bear nodded slowly, still considering how to handle this thing. He was not known for fairness, and now he was leaning toward Wolf Who Hunts Smiling's suggestion.

Now Spotted Tail too spoke up.

"Dismiss your troop, Lone Bear, or I swear I'll go to the Star Chamber!"

This was the final Cheyenne court of appeal, made up of six Headmen whose identities were known only to Chief Gray Thunder. They met in secret at the emergency request of respected war leaders. Their judgments outranked any others.

Lone Bear did not fear such an action. But it was clear that his men, with the exception of Wolf Who Hunts Smiling, were not eager to draw more blood from either Cheyenne.

"The punishment is terminated," he announced. "As for Little Horse, I have ears for those who plead his case. He will not be held in violation of the Hunt Law. But he and all others must remember—the law is strict on this point, that none may assist Touch the Sky. He has set himself outside of the tribe by his actions. Now he must suffer alone."

The braves were beginning to scatter when Touch the Sky's voice rang out. It was weak, strained from the injuries he'd received. But the words were clear enough even though spoken past bloodied, cut, and swollen lips.

"Wolf Who Hunts Smiling! After I saved you from the Pawnee, you vowed never to attempt to kill me again. But I would respect you more for killing me than for *this* cowardly sport! And so I warn you, best to kill me now, buck, or I will turn your guts into worm fodder."

Now Touch the Sky looked at Black Elk.

"And you, war leader! I used to call you my better. No more. Never mind what you have done here today to me! A man who would hit a woman, especially when she has done nothing to merit it, is merely a killer, not a true warrior.

"You once had honor, and I respected you for that. You no longer have it. And I warn you as I just warned your cousin, best to kill me now and have done with it. For truly I speak only one way, and I say this for all to know now. My father was a greater Cheyenne warrior than any man's here, and on his honor I swear it, both of you will pay for this."

A surprised silence greeted this announcement. This was the first time anyone, besides Arrow Keeper, had known anything about this supposed warrior father.

Black Elk, however, was enraged that this meddling squaw-stealer had publicly talked about his disciplining of his own wife!

"My father," he said, making the cutoff sign as one did when speaking of the dead, "died the glorious death at Wolf Creek. But only after he had smeared enemy blood over his entire body."

"And *my* father," Wolf Who Hunts Smiling said, "was killed by the paleface devils whose ways are in your blood."

"Both of us," Black Elk said, "have their weapons, their war bonnets, their enemy scalps on our lodgepoles. Can you produce these things that once belonged to your famous warrior father?"

This was greeted with laughter from the others. Soon everyone was mounting.

Touch the Sky spoke his final words on this matter. Little Horse could not believe his friend was still conscious after all this blood loss.

"I am not a sweet-talking Ponca who forgives his enemies. I tell you again, Black Elk and Wolf Who Hunts Smiling. Kill me now or sing the death song because I am *for* you!"

Chapter 8

While Touch the Sky lay helpless, the women and children moved the hunt camp to the dead buffalo. It was their job to do the bloody skinning and butchering.

The new temporary camp was a festive and noisy place. Hunters called out to each other, bragging, congratulating each other, acting out scenes from their kills. The women and children, lugging empty travois, were led to the animals killed by hunters in their clan.

The hides were stripped from head to buttocks. Then they were staked out flat to dry. Knives and stone chisels were used to scrape off every last bit of fat or flesh. Later, back at their permanent summer camp, the hides would be smoked over sweet grass to take out the smell.

Comanche Raid

The butchering was a bloody mess, and soon all the women, Honey Eater included, were covered with sticky blood from their hair to their moccasins. Drying racks had already been made out of mesquite branches. The women sliced most of the meat as thin as paper. Hung on the racks, it would be quickly dried by the Southwest sun and wind. It would remain edible for many moons.

Nothing was wasted. Other parts were set aside for the feast tonight at the dance of thanks for the good hunt. Blood and brains would be boiled together with rose hips to provide a true delicacy; the delicious tongues would be roasted so tender they would fall apart without chewing; the curdled, partially digested milk in the stomachs of the young buffalo calves was a treat many Indians dreamed about during the cold moons.

Everything they weren't consuming tonight would be piled onto the travois. Bones would yield tasty marrow; the horns of the bulls would provide cups; ropes and belts would be woven from the hair. Guts would soon string new bows; the kidney fat was stored in clay jars for cooking.

When the main job of butchering was finished, the hunt distribution was held.

This ancient Cheyenne custom ensured that sufficient fresh meat and delicacies would go to the elders and the poorest members of the tribe. The women of each clan had started a pile in a conspicuous place, contributing some of their clan's kill. When Chief Gray Thunder saw the pile, he ordered the soldier chiefs to take charge of the distribution.

83

Those who needed meat were already on hand. The soldiers set the meat up in equal piles. Then Spotted Tail of the Bowstrings selected River of Winds, known for his fair dealing, to inspect each pile and make sure they were equal. Then River of Winds made sure that no one was overlooked.

The soldiers were forced to turn away a woman from Swift Canoe's Wolverine Clan, though she protested loudly—she had already sent her daughter for a ration of meat, hiding it and getting in line herself.

Only after the soldiers reported the distribution complete did Gray Thunder order the dance of thanks to begin. Tonight they would feast; soon, when the meat was dried, they would move on after the herds. At least one more good kill was needed to see them through the cold moons.

Little Horse, like all the hunters, celebrated with his clan. But constantly he worried about Touch the Sky. However, the Bull Whips were making sure that no one went anywhere near the hunt transgressor. Hunt Law was strict on this point. Wolf Who Hunts Smiling especially kept his furtive, mocking eyes on Little Horse, daring him to violate the Hunt Law by helping his friend.

While the rest gorged themselves on fresh buffalo meat, many eating until they vomited, then eating more, Little Horse thought again with wonder of the thing Touch the Sky had claimed—that he was the son of a great Cheyenne warrior. This was the first Little Horse had heard of such a thing. He knew his friend too well by now to ever doubt his word.

Besides, Little Horse had glimpsed the mulberry-colored birthmark just past Touch the Sky's hairline, the perfect arrowhead shape. The traditional symbol of the warrior.

Earlier, Honey Eater had been clearly distraught when the women and children had been brought up to the site of the kill and she had realized Touch the Sky was not among the hunters. Little Horse, knowing he had to get word to her before she spotted the injured brave and rushed to him, took a great risk. He managed to get her aside for a moment, without being spotted by Black Elk, and explain the situation.

"How badly is he hurt?" she asked, alarm tightening her voice. She was kneeling over a hide, scraping fat away from it with a sharp-pointed stone chisel.

Little Horse, glancing around again to make sure Black Elk wasn't near, said, "He has been badly beaten, but he is strong. He has endured greater pain than this. He will survive. But it will be some time before he is able to move on his own."

"And Black Elk?" she said, her dark eyes snapping sparks. "Did he play the leader in this too?"

Little Horse glanced away, his silence answering her question for her.

"You say he has endured greater pain than this," Honey Eater said bitterly. "You speak true. Pain is all he has known since he joined our tribe. I am glad you are his friend, Little Horse."

"I am his friend until death, sister. But I can do nothing for him now."

Even covered head to toe with blood, her hair a ragged mass where Black Elk had cut her braid

85

off, Honey Eater was pretty. Little Horse thought again how natural it was that Touch the Sky would love her and she him. But the Cheyenne law-ways had forced her into a loveless marriage. And now Black Elk was making both of them suffer for their love.

They could risk no further conversation. Wolf Who Hunts Smiling was already riding over to see what was happening. Little Horse turned to leave. But Honey Eater called out his name. He turned back around.

Keeping her head down, continuing to scrape away at the staked-out hide, she said, "You know that I love him?"

"Yes. And I know that he loves you."

"Please do not let his enemies kill him!"

Wolf Who Hunts Smiling was almost upon them now, his knotted-thong whip cracking.

"If they do kill him," Little Horse vowed just before he left, "I swear by the four directions of the wind that my blood will run with his."

Touch the Sky lay where he had fallen beaten, unable to move, an outcast until he could ride on his own to camp. His weapons had been left alone, and his obedient pony grazed nearby without benefit of a tether.

For a long time—while his sister the sun slid across the sky—he lay dazed. His body alternated between dull throbbing and fiery pain. Awareness had become a narrow place surrounded by patches of dense fog. His mind passed from fog to clarity and back in an endless pattern. The skinning and butchering and feasting had gone on nearby with all the usual clamor. But to him it was all a dream, a thing of smoke.

His uncle the moon took over the sky, the long night passed, and the tribe moved out just after sunup of the new day. But Touch the Sky lay in utter exhaustion caused from enduring massive pain. However, even though the pain lanced deep into his flesh, his mind was freed as it had been on the Spirit Path at Medicine Lake. And once again images from his past were sprung from memory.

He glimpsed the unshaven, long-jawed face of Hiram Steele's wrangler Boone Wilson, again saw him unsheathing his Bowie knife while Steele's daughter Kristen screamed. He flexed another memory muscle, and now he saw the smug, overbearing sneer of Seth Carlson, the Blue-coat lieutenant who had helped Steele destroy the Hanchons' mercantile business.

There was more, images flying past like quick geese in a windstorm: He saw his own people torturing him over fire; saw the white whiskey trader again slaughtering white trappers and making the killings look "Indian"; saw himself counting coup on Seth Carlson when the officer tried to torch the Hanchon spread; saw the terrified Pawnees fleeing from Medicine Lake when he summoned a ferocious grizzly; saw the keelboat called the *Sioux Princess* exploding into splinters as he led his people to victory over the land-grabber Wes Munro during the already-famous Tongue River Battle.

And mixed in with all the fragments from his past were glimpses from his vision quest at Medicine Lake, glances stolen from the future: He saw his people freezing far to the north in the Land of the Grandmother, saw Cheyenne blood staining the snow. The screams of the dying ponies were even more hideous than the death cries of the Cheyenne.

It all led to one huge battle. And then the warrior leading the entire Cheyenne nation in its last great stand turned to utter the war cry, and Touch the Sky recognized the face under the long war bonnet as himself.

When all seems lost, Chief Yellow Bear's voice said to him again from the Land of Ghosts, *become your enemy!*

When he finally left the Spirit Path and woke to the life of the little day, the morning was well advanced. And now he felt the pain so intensely that he dared not move—every effort to do so sent a white-hot jolt through him and left him gasping.

The unjust beating had not left him humiliated. He had not been in the wrong. And did he not suffer in silence like a true warrior, only speaking to give his tormentors insults to answer their insults?

No, he told himself, his mouth a grim, determined slit against the pain, this was a matter of just revenge, not humiliation. He had meant what he told Black Elk and Wolf Who Hunts Smiling. Their lives were now forfeit. It was not just a matter of his own safety. Black Elk's jealousy was a worm cankering in his brain. In his insane rage, Black Elk would eventually do more to Honey Eater than cut off her braid.

Despite the sure knowledge that these things he was thinking were true things, Touch the Sky felt some sharp doubts pricking at him. The buffalo

hunt was at the very core of the Cheyenne way,
the basis for their very existence. Yet was this not
twice now that he had failed the hunt in some
way—his fault or not?

Had he not, after all, violated Hunt Law and
wasted good meat? Never mind the reasons and
excuses—the results could not be denied.

He knew that by now the tribe was moving on,
trailing the herd for the next kill. If—

Touch the Sky abruptly saw a harrowing sight
that scattered his thoughts like chaff in the
wind.

Fear moved up his spine in a cool tickle. Cresting the hills on the horizon, many riders strong,
was a large war party. Touch the Sky was too
far distant to make out their style of hair, by
which tribes could always be identified. But
almost surely in this area they would be Kiowa
or Comanche, probably both given their closeness
when it came to treading the warpath.

And these riders were definitely riding the warpath—so many streamered lances, easy to make
out in silhouette, could signify nothing else.

He clenched his jaw in frustrated helplessness
when he again tried to move. The effort made his
vision go dim with overwhelming pain.

And then the truth struck him with the force
of a blow. He was trapped, unable to even crawl
into hiding. If the war party kept advancing,
they would probably spot him and enjoy a bit
of unscheduled torture before they killed him.

Then they would move against the new hunt
camp, wherever it was established. Caught flush
in their hunt, the Cheyenne warriors, though
numerous, would be unpainted for battle, their

bonnets and shields unblessed. They would have no time to renew the Medicine Arrows for battle.

He recalled Arrow Keeper telling him the Kiowa and Comanche were zealous slave traders—especially in women and children. And he thought of Honey Eater and the suicide knife under her dress.

He was their only hope of an advance warning. Again, desperation warring with the pain, he tried to sit up. But his tortured flesh seemed to scream its pain, and his mind shut down to darkness.

Chapter 9

Hairy Wolf halted the column of warriors in the lee of a long ridge.

"We camp here," the big Kiowa told Iron Eyes.

His Comanche friend nodded. "This is a good place. We can make small fires, and if they send scouts behind to check on their back trail, we will not be spotted."

Hairy Wolf reined his pony around. His bone breastplate gleamed brightly in the late afternoon sun. He signaled for the best scouts, Stone Mountain and Kicking Bird, to ride forward.

"Ride on ahead," he told them, "and discover where the next hunt camp is located. As soon as you know when the hunters will be going out again, race back with the word."

"Move like coyotes through prairie chickens," Iron Eyes added. "They must *not* spot you. We want the women and children left alone in camp."

While the scouts rode out, the Comanche named Dog Fat returned from a quick check just forward of their present position.

"The Cheyenne are long gone. But there is a fine gray pony grazing by itself, untethered, near the sight of their first butchering. I want to ride closer and see if it is for the taking."

Dog Fat had not noticed the injured Cheyenne brave lying in the knee-deep buffalo grass not far from the pony.

Iron Eyes considered his request. "You are sure it is not simply another one of their clever false camps?"

"No one would leave this fine pony in a false camp as a lure," Dog Fat said with conviction. "And it is rigged for riding. I think something happened to its rider, and it is for the taking."

Iron Eyes looked at Hairy Wolf. His friend nodded once. Dog Fat, known for his love of torturing captives, was also a capable buck with a reputation for superior stealth. It might be useful to have a look around the area of the Cheyenne's last camp.

"Go then," Iron Eyes said. "But be all eyes and ears."

Dog Fat loosened the lead line tied to his buffalo-hide saddle. Then he brandished his stone skull-cracker. "If I set eyes on a Cheyenne, he will never make another track."

92

Comanche Raid

* * *

Touch the Sky felt like he was floating up toward the surface of a river, rising faster and faster like an air bubble. Then suddenly he broke surface, and his eyes snapped open.

The afternoon sunlight was hot on his face. For a moment he remembered nothing, did not know where he was or how he got there. Then he tried to sit up. The abrupt jolt of pain brought him back to the present, and he remembered the war party.

This time he did manage to sit up, though the pain made his eyes water. He could move a little easier now. But why was he even still alive? The war party surely could not have missed him when it passed by.

But they must have. Somehow, though he was stiff and bloodied and raw from his beating, he had to race on and warn the tribe. By now they were almost a full sleep's ride ahead of him.

He had just screwed up his courage to attempt rising from the ground when he glimpsed a lone rider approaching from the ridge on the horizon. He lowered himself again into the waving buffalo grass. Spotting the gray made him realize that the war party could not have ridden past. Even if they had missed him, quite possible in the grass, they would not have left his pony.

In fact, clearly it was his pony this lone brave was interested in now.

His curiosity was mixed with a feeling of sick dread. What did this enemy have planned? If they meant to engage Cheyenne warriors in a fight, why halt their advance now so early? The Comanche especially were known for attacking at night. So why weren't they following the tribe, moving into position to strike?

Unless they had something else in mind—some opportunity they planned to seize when the Cheyenne braves were all distracted by the hunt.

Some opportunity which these infamous slave-takers would seize in the hunt camp itself, not on the battlefield.

But now there was no more time to speculate. The rider was close enough for Touch the Sky to recognize that he was definitely Comanche. He was heavy but strong, a roll of fat hanging over the top of a pair of filthy Army trousers with yellow piping down the sides. His hair was parted exactly in the center and tucked back behind his ears. He carried a stone war club resting across one thigh.

And he was definitely intent on capturing the gray. As he drew closer, he looked cautiously all around. Touch the Sky, wincing at the movement, ducked even lower.

His rifle was still in the scabbard sewn to his horse blanket. His lance and throwing ax too were lashed to his pony. The only weapon left to him was the obsidian knife in his beaded sheath. He slid it out now, even that simple movement sending hot explosions of pain into his limbs.

The Comanche halted his buckskin pony and dismounted, uncoiling the lead line as he moved closer to the gray. The gray shied and nickered, moving off a few paces.

Touch the Sky's brain raced, searching for a way out of this threatened loss of his horse. He himself was safe for now, but what good was safety on the Plains without a horse? In his condition, he was as good as dead.

The fat Comanche moved in again. Again the gray nickered and trotted off. But the Comanche obviously had experience with horses. He continued speaking to it gently as he moved in, soothing it.

The brave wasn't looking in his direction now. Touch the Sky rose to his knees again, pain screaming from every pore of his whip-lashed body. The Comanche was actually singing to the gray now, a low, soothing song in words Touch the Sky couldn't understand. But the song had a lulling effect on the pony. She finally stood still as the Comanche moved in close enough to slip the lead line through her hackamore.

Trembling with the effort, Touch the Sky drew his right hand back behind his head. As the intruder began to lead his pony back to his own mount, Touch the Sky threw the knife in a fast overhand throw. The exertion made him gasp with pain.

But his aim was true. The knife punched into the Comanche's back just behind the heart, dropping him to his knees. A moment later he dropped forward onto his face, legs twitching in death agony.

Touch the Sky set his lips in a grim, determined slit and rose shakily to his feet. It cost a great effort, but he managed to cross to the dead Comanche and jerk his knife from his back. He wiped the blade in the grass and slid the weapon back into its sheath.

The gray nuzzled his shoulder, glad to see him on his feet again. It made hot red waves of pain wash over him, but in a few moments he was mounted. He glanced once toward the long ridge behind him, then stared out across the parched expanse in the direction his people had ridden. It was a vast vista of redrock canyons and arroyos, of steep mesas and buttes and sandstone rises.

Reading their trail would be no challenge, not with all those travois heavily laden with meat. But was there time to catch them and warn them? If Kiowas or Comanches on their notoriously fleet-footed ponies spotted him, he knew he could never outrun them—certainly not in his present condition.

But he had no choice. It was either do it or don't do it. And if he didn't do it, Gray Thunder's tribe was surely in great danger. This Comanche was no lone spy sent to gather information. He was part of a powerful war party.

Nor could Touch the Sky be sure he would ride out of this place alive. He had no exact idea where the rest of the enemy might be camped. Perhaps they were keeping an eye on him at this very moment.

Trying not to glance at his blood-encrusted wounds, Touch the Sky nudged his pony's flanks and set out in search of his tribe.

When Dog Fat did not return in a reasonable time, his friend Standing Feather accompanied Iron Eyes and Hairy Wolf to learn what had delayed him.

He was still barely breathing when they found him, bloody foam bubbling on his lips. Even as

Standing Feather turned him onto his back, the death rattle rose in his throat with a noise like pebbles shaken in a shaman's dried gourd.

His face grim, Standing Feather performed the Comanche death ritual. "Father in heaven," he intoned, "this, our brother, is coming." Then, embracing the dying man, he flapped his hands behind him like wings while he imitated an eagle's call. Thus Dog Fat's soul would be flown to heaven.

While Standing Feather lashed his dead companion to his horse, Hairy Wolf gazed off in the direction Touch the Sky had recently ridden out. The Kiowa chief looked for a long time, as if reading some clue on the distant horizon. His eyes squeezed to slits as they stared into the setting sun.

Iron Eyes knew perfectly well what he was thinking. After all, it was the Comanches who had perfected the tactic of attacking out of the sun.

"I do not relish riding into the sun," Hairy Wolf finally said. "But neither can we stay. Surely it was a Cheyenne who killed Dog Fat. He could not have much of a lead. Never mind our fine camp. I say we ride now and reach the Cheyenne before this dog's barking alerts his fellow warriors."

"Tienes razon," Iron Eyes said in Spanish. "You are right. And when we catch him, we will feed his own eyes to him."

By nightfall Touch the Sky realized his enemies were closing in on him.

The gray was well rested from her long graze. But Touch the Sky could not constantly hold a fast pace. The jarring and bouncing felt like more whips—dozens of them—flailing him raw all over again.

Each time he crested a ridge, he glanced back and spotted his dogged pursuers closing the gap. Clearly there would not be enough time to warn the tribe.

Fear and frustration vied with the excruciating pain of bouncing on his pony. Several of the deeper whip cuts were bleeding afresh, and occasionally he tasted blood running into his mouth or was forced to swipe at his eyes to clear his vision.

As he clung to his mount, trying to place the pain outside of himself as Arrow Keeper had taught him to do, he thought of a desperate plan. It might well get him killed. But otherwise, Gray Thunder's tribe was in serious trouble.

Touch the Sky knew his trail was being lost in the much larger path left by his tribe. When he reached an arroyo that ran at right angles to the trail, he leaped the obedient gray into it and doubled back around. Riding behind a huge, sloping rise, he hurried into position behind the war party.

As he had hoped they would, the combined band of Kiowa and Comanche warriors made a brief stop to eat and water their ponies in a clear tributary of the Brazos River. While they prepared their meals of parched corn and a thick soup made from the paste of crushed insects, their ponies were hobbled in a group at the water's edge.

Touch the Sky rode his own pony as close as he dared. Then, grimacing at the throbbing pain, he dismounted and tethered his gray behind a thick stand of Spanish Bayonet. It was nearly dark now. But he knew darkness would not deter either tribe from moving and attacking. The pain making his entire body protest, he leapfrogged from cottonwood to cottonwood, from prickly pear to prickly pear, moving ever closer to the hobbled ponies.

Small groups of braves were scattered about everywhere, cooking over small fires. At times Touch the Sky could find no cover. Then he was forced to simply crawl along the ground and pray to Maiyun that he would not be spotted. Sweat broke out all over his body and streamed into his cuts, causing a fiery, itching sting.

Finally he reached the horses.

Moving quickly despite the pain, he began untying the short rawhide hobbles. He prayed that none of the horses would move enough to capture enemy attention, at least not before he had freed plenty of them.

This night Maiyun was with him. He had untied nearly half of the horses before any of them began moving very far. Knowing he had reached the most dangerous moment of his plan, he abruptly shouted the shrill Cheyenne war cry as he slapped the nearest ponies on the flanks.

"Hi-ya, hii-ya!"

Only a few heartbeats later the frightened mounts were scattering across the shallow tributary and out onto the flat.

In the confusion he was able to slip away and return to his pony. Cutting well around the tumult of the campsite, he urged the gray onward. He knew his enemies would lose valuable time recovering their ponies. But would it be enough time? he wondered.

And even as he asked the question, he also answered it: He had done all he could. It would *have* to be enough time.

Chapter 10

All through the night Touch the Sky pushed his horse as hard as he possibly could, stopping only to make sure he was still on the trail of Gray Thunder's tribe.

He was numb now to the pain. After his sister the sun had gone to her resting place, the night air had cooled considerably and soothed his pain-ravaged skin. A three-quarter moon and a star-shot sky made visibility good and fast riding easy.

He ate while he rode, chewing on the pemmican and dried plums in his legging sash. Each time he stopped to verify the trail, he knelt and placed his ear close to the ground, listening for sounds of pursuit. He heard nothing, but this hardly reassured him. The Kiowas and

Comanches were famous for their stealth—often, only one scout would actually follow behind an enemy, the rest riding well to the flanks and using lone riders to stay in touch with him. This way their quarry might relax and easily be taken by surprise. Every Cheyenne knew the famous stories about Comanches stealing up to sleeping couples so quietly they could kidnap the wife without waking the husband or her.

So Touch the Sky did not relax his vigilance. He was still riding hard when dawn finally painted the eastern sky in roseate hues.

Despite his pain and fear for the tribe, Touch the Sky could not help being filled with wonder at the grand beauty of this Southwest canyon country. Mountains never seemed close, yet in every direction he looked they raised their white-capped peaks into the sky above the distant horizons. Startled roadrunners scurried in front of his horse, and huge tumbleweeds bounced and hopped and rolled with incredible speed. Everywhere majestic cactus formations stood out against the sky. Some bore uncanny resemblance to human figures.

Grass was not as plentiful as it was on the Plains to the north. But neither were white hunters, blue-dressed soldiers, and paleface work crews stringing the talking wires which carried words through the air like bolts of lightning. As a result, game had become more plentiful in this semiarid country. Toward mid-morning Touch the Sky glimpsed a herd of antelope, their white-spotted flanks flashing in the sun.

In daylight the churned-up earth caused by the buffalo herd was easier to follow than a paleface wagon road. It was shedding season; occasionally, near water, he would encounter cottonwood trees, their thick-ridged bark covered with woolly hair where the buffalos had backed against them to scratch themselves.

Finally, riding up out of a shallow red-dirt ravine, he spotted the conical tipis of the temporary Cheyenne hunt camp.

He saw at his very first glance that the men were gone. Clearly they had already ridden further forward for the next kill. This troubled Touch the Sky. Had Arrow Keeper and Gray Thunder and the rest been present, he could have warned them that an enemy war party was near, probably approaching.

Now he would almost surely have to convince whoever was in charge of the hunt camp to pack it up and go forward, joining the hunters for safety even earlier than Hunt Law dictated. This could jeopardize the hunt by frightening off the buffalo. But if they were indeed in danger of attack, his action would not cause him trouble with the headmen. However, if enemy pursuers failed to show up, he would be in trouble yet again.

Still, he thought, thinking of Honey Eater, the risk was worth it.

Then, as he topped the last long rise before entering camp, he realized there would be no chance to join the hunters. He had turned to look behind him one last time. And there, on the distant horizon, he saw a brown cloud of dust swirling above the ground—riders approaching fast. The attack was coming.

How many? he wondered. Could they have captured their horses so quickly they were able to
catch him like this? It didn't seem likely, as hard
as he had been riding. More likely, they had sent
a smaller force on the horses Touch the Sky had
not been able to scatter. He hoped this last was
the case.

And now his suspicions became a certainty:
This was not strictly a war party, but a slave-
taking mission. The Kiowas and their Comanche
allies were especially fond of the Cheyennes
because the Beautiful People brought a good
price in guns and bullets and alcohol and the
white man's rich tobacco. And Honey Eater
might very well end up in one of Santa Fe's or
Chihuahua's stinking bordellos.

As he entered the camp, the women and children and elders eyed him curiously. They knew
he had been punished by the Bull Whips. Yet
very few respected the Whips, so their eyes
were sympathetic when they saw his wounds.
The warriors-in-training, who had between 12
and 15 winters behind them, had been left in
charge of the camp. They too eyed him curiously,
many with open respect—though he was called a
troublemaker and a white man's dog, all knew of
his feats as a warrior. They had counted the coup
feathers in his war bonnet, remarked on the mass
of scars covering his chest and back.

"Little Brother!" Touch the Sky called out to a
junior warrior named Stump Horn. "Who is in
charge?"

"Two Twists," the youth replied.

"Run quickly and get him. You are about to
taste your first fight!"

The youth's dark eyes widened at this news. He tore off to find Two Twists. Meantime, drawn out of her tipi by the sound of his voice, Honey Eater crossed quickly toward Touch the Sky as he dismounted.

She stopped dead in her tracks, however, when she saw what the savage whipping had done to his flesh. Before she spoke even a word, her eyes filmed with tears.

"Is this what my husband the Bull Whip has done to you? *This?* Little Horse told me they hurt you, but this!"

The words choked her throat and she turned her head away, tears now openly streaming down her cheeks.

"It was not enough," she added bitterly, "that they beat you this way. Black Elk and Wolf Who Hunts Smiling are also saying things. They say you should not be allowed on this or any other hunt because your smell is scaring away the herds."

"To you I will say nothing against your husband," Touch the Sky said. "I will settle with him and his lying cousin, all in good time. For now, little Honey Eater, dry your tears and draw on your courage as a Cheyenne woman—an attack is coming!"

At this news the sadness left her face, replaced by the same grim determination that now marked his scarred features. Now Two Twists was rapidly approaching from the opposite end of camp.

As they waited for the youth, Touch the Sky hungrily drank in a long glance at the woman he loved with all his soul. Rarely did he get an opportunity to be this close to her without having

105

to worry about Black Elk's jealous eyes.

She flushed under his stare, turning her face away. "I am ashamed to have you see me like this."

He knew she was talking about her mangled hair.

"A beautiful oak," he said, "is the same tree even after its leaves blow away during the cold moons. And soon, the new leaves grow back."

Despite the danger approaching, his words brought a brief smile to her face. But now Two Twists had arrived.

"Little brother," Touch the Sky said, "how long would it take to move the women and children to the hunt?"

"Perhaps half a morning's ride."

This news made Touch the Sky frown.

"Then we must stand and hold," Touch the Sky said. "Kiowas and Comanches are approaching even now and will catch us if we try to flee. Gather all your warriors, buck."

Two Twists, who had earned his name from his preference for wearing his hair in two braids instead of just one, which was the usual custom, swelled with importance at these words. He nodded and raced off to gather the bucks.

"Honey Eater," Touch the Sky added, "gather the women and elders. We must make our battle plan, and quickly. I fear these red devils are not coming simply to fight. They plan to steal women and children as slaves!"

Touch the Sky knew their enemy was approaching rapidly, so the impromptu council was brief.

Comanche Raid

As always when the tribe was traveling, the women had brought along their stone-bladed hoes which they used to dig up wild turnips and onions. At Touch the Sky's instructions, they went to work digging shallow rifle pits in the loose soil. He had come up with a reckless plan which might well get him killed. But Touch the Sky knew full well it was their only chance.

The young warriors had no time to paint or dress for battle. Unlike some tribes, which rode into battle on a moment's notice, the Cheyenne tribe always painted their faces and donned special battle garb. This was considered so important that, often, courageous warriors fled from a fight if they could not thus prepare.

But fleeing, and deserting the women and children, was out of the question now. So Two Twists went around to all the junior warriors, quickly marking their faces with black charcoal—the symbol of joy in the death of an enemy.

Then, while Honey Eater and the other young women gathered up all the children, Touch the Sky addressed Two Twists and the rest of the youths.

"Little brothers! Hear my words and place them in your sashes. Soon the war cry will sound, and blood will stain the earth. True it is you are young. But every great warrior was once young. I watched my brother Little Horse wade into the midst of frenzied Pawnees when he had only fifteen winters behind him, like Two Twists here. And I swear by the earth we live on, my brother greased their bones with his war paint!

"Little brothers! Of course you feel fear at this moment. So do I, and have you counted my

107

scalps? There is nothing unmanly in feeling fear. It is staying and doing that counts! We are the fighting Cheyenne! Remember this, you do not fight for glory or for scalps or for the right to stand in the doorway of the clan lodges and make brags. You fight to save your mothers, your grandparents, the little ones who are the future of the Cheyenne people."

The youths were stone silent, stone still, absorbing every word. This Touch the Sky, had he not counted first coup at the famous Tongue River Battle which saved their homeland from greedy whites?

It was a rare mark of distinction for a warrior such as this to address them as fighters, as brothers. Yes, they were afraid. But their games from infancy on had all centered around mock battles, taking scalps, and counting coups. Two of them had even lost an eye from "toy" arrows fired from miniature bows in battle. They were afraid, but they were keen to prove themselves.

"Bucks, this day you will cover your tribe in glory! If you fall, fall on the bones of a Kiowa or Comanche. If their blood be rain, cause a flash flood! The Cheyenne tribe defeated them at Wolf Creek. Some of your fathers were in that battle when they were barely older than you are today. What Cheyennes have done, Cheyennes will do!"

Now Touch the Sky thrust his war lance over his head.

"Hi-ya!" he screamed. *"Hii-ya!"*

As one, the junior warriors repeated the war cry.

"One bullet!" Touch the Sky shouted.

"One enemy!" the warriors responded.

"One bullet!"

"One enemy!"

They were worked up to a frenzy, their eyes blazing.

"Quickly now," Touch the Sky said. "Make ready your battle rigs. And never forget, the fight is not over until the last Cheyenne buck is dead. I have spoken and can say no more. From this moment forth, let deeds speak for words. Two Twists, take command of your warriors."

Hurriedly, Two Twists began issuing orders while Touch the Sky headed quickly to a spot just north of camp. It had caught his eye because of a series of small humps on the ground, humps that could not be seen easily from horseback.

Sure enough, it turned out to be an area pocked with holes left by prairie dogs. Touch the Sky saw that he could stand behind it and still be close enough to call out commands to the warriors in the rifle pits just to his right and behind him. He would be completely exposed, but that was part of the plan.

The dust cloud on the eastern horizon was beginning to take shape now. Touch the Sky gave thanks to the four directions and to Maiyun, the Good Supernatural, when he realized this force was only about half the size of the original war party he had spotted—meaning that only those whose horses he had not scattered had come after him.

Still, even so, there were at least three Comanche and Kiowa attackers for every young Cheyenne defender. It was not just a brave rallying cry—it really *would* have to be one bullet, one enemy, or they would be overrun in mere moments.

Before he walked back to the main camp, he dropped to his knees and briefly offered a battle prayer. Already, he could hear Two Twists leading the youths in a Cheyenne battle song to fortify their courage.

Now it was time to return and give them their final instructions.

By now Honey Eater and the others had gathered the children and elderly behind a hastily erected breastwork. She knew by now that the attackers were Kiowa and Comanche—and she also knew what that meant.

Unaware that he was observing her, Honey Eater's right hand rose to touch the rawhide thong of the suicide knife hidden under the neck of her doeskin dress. If the attack went badly, he knew the women would try to kill the children and themselves before they allowed the slave-takers to grab them.

Then Honey Eater saw him watching her.

She lifted both hands and crossed her wrists in front of her heart—Cheyenne sign talk for love.

Out on the horizon, the boiling, yellow-brown dust cloud drew closer and closer.

Chapter 11

Two Twists and the other junior warriors had settled into the rifle pits and readied their weapons. Fortunately, the Cheyenne beaver traps had yielded a good supply of pelts this season, and the tribe was well equipped with rifles, ball, and black powder.

Touch the Sky walked up and down among the pits, calming the youths, inspecting weapons, repeating his instructions over and over. He knew that, caught flush in the heat of battle, the brain could sometimes shut down completely and cause serious mistakes.

His plan revolved around the words Arrow Keeper had spoken to him before the hunt:

I have seen Comanches when their ponies are shot out from under them. It is said they lose their courage when not on horseback.

The fierce warriors *must* be separated from their mounts. The number-one priority this time was neither counting coup nor even killing their enemies—they must simply prevent them from ever getting past the line of defenders. A thin line made up of Touch the Sky and a dozen or so unblooded warriors was all that protected the women and children and elders.

Touch the Sky had already borrowed Two Twist's war shield made from the sturdy wood of an osage tree. It would stop arrows, but not bullets. He could only hope the attackers were not rich in firearms and bullets, for his part in the plan would call for constant exposure to the attackers.

For this reason, he also removed the mountain-lion skin tucked into the pannier sewn to his horse blanket. Arrow Keeper had given it to him, assuring him it was blessed with strong medicine. Little Horse swore that, while he was wearing it during the Tongue River Battle, it had made a load of musket balls fired from a blunderbuss miss him at point-blank range. Touch the Sky donned it now, not sure if he believed or not. But he did believe in Arrow Keeper's magic—had in fact witnessed it numerous times.

By now the hollow thundering of hooves clearly reached the camp as the attackers drew ever closer. Touch the Sky returned to his position just to the left, and in front of, the rifle pits and the camp.

"Stay out of sight!" he called out again to the junior warriors when one of them peeked anxiously over the top of his pit. "I will be your eyes.

They must not see you. If they do, they will go into a circular attack, and then all is lost."

In fact, Touch the Sky feared this might happen anyway. If it did, his plan to use himself as a lure would be useless. It was necessary to convince the attackers that he was the only defender and trick them into a direct assault. He knew the Kiowa and Comanche would prefer this, not wishing to give the Cheyenne women time to use their suicide knives.

"Steady, little brothers!" he called out again. "Heads down! You know what you must do. We are the fighting Cheyenne!"

He was forced to speak even louder now above the noise of the ponies and the shrill war cries of the Comanche and Kiowa. He could make them out clearly now, racing through the flowering mescal and low-hanging pods of mesquite. Their leader was a huge Kiowa with a bone breastplate and a flowing black mane of hair streaming behind him.

"Two Twists!" Touch the Sky shouted above the din.

"Yes!"

"A pure black with white forelegs, bearing straight down on you. It is their war leader's pony."

"I am *for* him!"

The first sharp cracks of the attackers' rifles sounded. Bullets whipped past Touch the Sky's ears with a sound like angry hornets. Holding the shield in his left hand, Touch the Sky lifted his Sharps into the socket of his right shoulder and snapped off a round. As he had hoped, this seemed to focus the attackers' attention squarely on him.

"Walking Coyote!"

"I hear you, Touch the Sky!"

"A buckskin, bearing down just to my left! Wait for the command."

"Already dead!" the youth shouted back.

More rifles cracked, a chip flew from Touch the Sky's shield. The first arrows had already embedded themselves in the sturdy wood.

"Stump Horn!"

"Here, brother!"

"A small chestnut on the far right flank!"

"My aim will be true!" the youth replied.

Now the attackers were closing fast. More chips flew from the war shield, and an arrow flew past his exposed right leg so close that the fletching burned his skin. Touch the Sky could clearly make out the painted horses, distinguish the oval-faced Comanches with their green and yellow war paint from the Kiowa faces painted in garish greens and yellows and reds.

"Young Two Moons!"

"I have ears!"

"A pure ginger with a tan mane!"

"I will leave it for the Apaches to eat!"

And thus it went, Touch the Sky calling out the junior warriors' names one by one, calming them while also telling them exactly which horse was their target so that each shot might count.

The arrows were coming in with more accuracy now, and Touch the Sky tried to hunch himself into a smaller target behind the shield. A bullet ripped through the parfleche on his sash. Despite the danger now pressing down on him, Touch the

Comanche Raid

Sky could not help admiring the skill of the riders. The Comanches especially seemed to blend with their horses. They did not even bother to hold on—they strung arrows and reloaded their rifles, which thankfully were not as plentiful as bows, as easily as if they were sitting on the ground.

A bullet pierced the shield and almost knocked it from Touch the Sky's hand. Now the enemy was so close he could see the blood lust in their eyes.

"Steady, little brothers! Steady! One shot, and you must make it count."

The Comanches liked to capture Bluecoat bugles in battles with the pony soldiers, then blow them to mock their enemies. Now, celebrating what was clearly about to be an easy victory, one of them sounded a bad version of "Boots and Saddles."

A flurry of arrows rattled into the shield and were shot between his legs. Another corner of the shield was chipped away.

"NOW, Cheyennes!" Touch the Sky bellowed above the din.

As one man, the dozen young warriors rose from their rifle pits and fired together. Immediately, at least ten ponies collapsed. This took the thunder out of the enemy war cries and silenced the bugler, who found himself bruised and shaken on the ground with many of his comrades.

But though the attack was considerably slowed, the rest continued charging toward Touch the Sky. However, he had timed his command to come just before the survivors would reach the stretch of ground pocked with prairie-dog holes. They entered it now, and several ponies tripped hard, throwing their whooping riders earthward.

One pony, ridden by a Comanche on a captured cavalry saddle, quickly struggled back up and bolted off to the right. The rider was trapped with one foot twisted in the stirrup. The panicked mount raced directly through a patch of sturdy, sharp-needled prickly-pear cactus, dragging the rider behind. The Comanche's screams were hideous as the needles turned him into a raw, red, glistening mess, literally skinning him alive.

His screaming death agony finally unnerved the attackers. Stopping only long enough to let their brothers whose horses had been shot leap up behind them, they retreated.

A triumphant victory cry rose from the young warriors in the rifle pits, and was taken up by the noncombatants huddled behind the breastworks.

But Touch the Sky, though elated by this temporary victory, was not lulled into a sense of security. Of all the tribes whose treachery could not be predicted, Arrow Keeper had often told him, the Kiowa and Comanche were the most dangerous.

There was no time for a celebration. This was only half of the combined enemy force. And only one had died here today. This was their homeland, and fresh remounts would not be far off.

Another attack, a far bigger one, would soon be coming.

Touch the Sky, assisted by Two Twists, supervised the move as the camp was once again dismantled to join the hunters. He had no idea when the next attack was coming. But he feared it would be soon. Although the strict Hunt Law required the camp to wait until it was summoned, the delay couldn't be risked.

Tipi covers and poles, cooking utensils, drying racks, and other possessions were lashed to travois along with the dried meat and other parts of the buffalo already killed. Thus weighted down, the camp could not make such good time as the unencumbered hunters had. As always, flankers were sent out, selected from the junior warriors, as well as a guard to ride behind in case the attacking band should decide on an immediate second strike.

Touch the Sky's numerous cuts had finally scabbed over, a dull itching replacing the burning pain. Still, he was nearly exhausted from the ordeal of his beating and the all-night ride to warn the camp in time. Only the thought that Honey Eater and the rest depended on him kept him going. So far, not one drop of Cheyenne blood had been spilled. It was his responsibility, as the only full warrior in the group, to make sure that none was.

He was proud of Two Twists and his warriors. The youths had played their parts well, had followed orders exactly. So he wisely held silent now as they puffed themselves up with pride, boasting to each other as warriors will do. Around the women and children, however, they showed the taciturn reserve of the older Cheyenne braves— after all, had they not fired upon an enemy in battle? It was no longer acceptable to act like children.

And they looked toward Touch the Sky with a new respect in their eyes. Each of them had watched him stand and hold in an uncovered position while enemy arrows and bullets rained down upon him. The elders and the women smiled shyly each time he met their eyes, admiration clear in their manner. Touch the Sky did not know it yet, but the same old squaw of the Sky Walker Clan who had sung the song about his love for Honey Eater was already composing another about his bravery this day. Soon it too would be sung in the clan circles and lodges and become part of the history of the Cheyenne people.

But wisely, Touch the Sky now kept his distance from Honey Eater as they rode. The two could not be near each other without showing their powerful love. And despite Touch the Sky's bravery, Black Elk's friends and informers were numerous.

The sun was a flaming red ball balanced on the western horizon by the time they reached the spot where the hunters had congregated. The hunters spotted them as they emerged over a long ridge. The herd could be seen far below in a grassy valley of the Red River. Clearly the kill had not yet taken place. No doubt, thought Touch the Sky, it was planned for sunrise.

Although they were approaching against the wind, Touch the Sky halted his column well back from the hunters and waited for a delegation to approach.

Their faces incredulous at this clear violation of Hunt Law, the Bull Whips raced out ahead of Chief Gray Thunder and Arrow Keeper. They were led by Lone Bear and Black Elk, Wolf Who Hunts Smiling close on their heels.

"You!" Lone Bear said. "What is the meaning of this outrage? You know full well the people must

be left behind until after the kill or the herd may be scared off."

Touch the Sky was about to speak when Two Twists rode boldly forward.

"Fathers! I am young, but today I fought in my first battle. Please have ears for my words. Touch the Sky has the courage of ten warriors! This day he saved Gray Thunder's tribe from a terrible tragedy."

Clearly, emboldened by his part in the fight, Two Twists narrated the events of the attack. Gray Thunder and Arrow Keeper rode up as he told the story and listened attentively. Some of the women and elders crowded closer as Two Twists spoke, nodding excitedly. "Yes, this is surely true!" they said, or, "Yes, I saw him do that!"

By the time Two Twists finished and fell silent, Gray Thunder was staring at Touch the Sky with respect clear in his eyes. Old Arrow Keeper too gazed at the youth fondly, nodding his head as if this were to be expected from a youth who carried the mark of the warrior on his scalp. Little Horse, his face proud, glanced around at the others as if to say: *Do you mark this? This is my brother, the warrior!*

Black Elk, Lone Bear, and Wolf Who Hunts Smiling, however, exchanged troubled glances.

"Father," Touch the Sky said to Gray Thunder, "I took it upon myself to move the camp early because I am convinced our enemies plan another strike, a bigger strike with many more warriors. It is only a matter of time."

Gray Thunder nodded. "You were right to do so."

Now the chief glanced with disapproval at Lone Bear and Black Elk. "It was the responsibility of our soldier societies and our battle chief to make sure our women and children and elders were better protected. Fortunately, our young calves turned into raging bulls under Touch the Sky's brave example."

Lone Bear, Black Elk, and Wolf Who Hunts Smiling chaffed under this criticism.

"But Father!" Wolf Who Hunts Smiling protested. "Touch the Sky ruined the first hunt. He has the stink on him. He should leave before the herds smell him."

"He will stay," Gray Thunder said firmly, brooking no argument. "Every instinct now tells me he was unfairly accused and whipped. I know that Hunt Law leaves this matter up to Lone Bear and Spotted Tail, leaders of the soldier troops who police the hunts. But I swear by my medicine bundle, I will convene the Star Chamber and override them if they fight me on this point!"

Neither troop leader spoke up to object. A Cheyenne chief could not dictate to his people—he was the voice of the tribe, not its will. But Gray Thunder was still, in his fortieth winter, a vigorous warrior and highly respected for the eagle feathers in his war bonnet.

"We will post guards all about," the chief continued, "and we will renew the Medicine Arrows for battle just in case Touch the Sky is right and the attack is coming. But tomorrow the hunt goes on as we planned. It is too important to our tribe. Shaman!"

He turned to Arrow Keeper.

"Prepare the Sacred Arrows. Tonight the warriors will make their offerings. Then, tomorrow, they will paint and dress before the kill. Thus we will be ready if the attack comes to us."

Gray Thunder looked at Two Twists, a smile touching his stern features. "And tomorrow, Two Twists and the junior warriors who saved our people will ride in the hunt with the blooded warriors."

A cheer rose from the warriors-in-training. But Touch the Sky watched Black Elk and Wolf Who Hunts Smiling exchange a long, conspiratorial look, and he knew that more trouble was in the wind.

Chapter 12

Hairy Wolf finished smoking and laid the long clay pipe on the ground between himself and Iron Eyes. This signified that he was now ready to speak.

"They shot my best pony out from under me," he said with bitter humiliation. "All of our warriors witnessed it. Those were *children* who made a brave warrior, a member of the Kaitsenko, show the white feather and flee! Am I a Kiowa, or a cowardly Ponca who grows gardens and preaches peace?"

He and Iron Eyes sat apart from the rest of their band, faces grim and hatchet-sharp in profile in the flickering orange flames of a small camp fire.

"I hear this, Kaitsenko," Iron Eyes said. "When

they first drove us Comanches to this land, there were no buffalo herds here. The hair mouths had not yet diverted the herds south. We were finally forced to kill and eat our dogs, then our ponies. This thing today, it will not stand."

"It will not," Hairy Wolf agreed. "The runners report that our braves who were delayed capturing their ponies will soon arrive. And I have already sent a loaded pipe to He Bear and his band. Count upon it, he will respond quickly. No man alive has more reason to hate the Shaiyena than He Bear. True it is, we will be forced to split with him the goods we receive from the slave sale. But the price is well worth it."

Just south of their present camp lived the Kiowa Apaches, close kin to the Kiowa, under their war leader He Bear. Each fall, during the Deer-rutting Moon, various tribes of the Southern Plains assembled in conclave at Medicine Lodge Creek in the heartland of the Kiowas. Almost all of these tribes had been driven from the north by combined Cheyenne-Sioux might. Thus the Cheyennes had become their hereditary enemies.

"This year," Hairy Wolf said, "at Medicine Lodge Creek, He Bear complained bitterly about Cheyennes raiding on his pony herds. But his band is too small to attack in revenge. This will be a perfect chance to exact blood justice against them. Our three tribes will raise our battle-axes as one."

All evening both leaders had carefully avoided mentioning a certain name which was much on their minds. The Comanche killed in that prickly pear patch had been Painted Lips, one of the favorites of both bands. But by Comanche custom, a warrior whose body had not been recovered could never be mentioned again.

"Yes," Iron Eyes said, "we will attack as one. I like this. It is worth surrendering some of our profits from the slaves. Because now we can do more than simply sneak up and steal women and children—we will also annihilate their warriors!"

"Brother," Little Horse said, "I am proud of you. Do you know that old Sweet Medicine of the Sky Walker Clan has composed a song honoring your bravery? All of the young warriors are singing your praise, telling how a lone Cheyenne brave stood before an entire band of Kiowa and Comanches and never once flinched at their arrows and bullets."

"I flinched, brother," Touch the Sky said, though indeed he was proud to hear such words from Little Horse, his best friend and the warrior he admired most in his tribe. "It was our tribe behind me which held me fast, not my contempt for death."

"I have no ears for this. But bend words anyway you wish. Deeds hold only one shape, and your deeds today have the shape of courage. My young sisters and brothers were among those children, my uncles and aunts and grandparents among the elders. We are warriors, and I will not embarrass you by dwelling upon this thing longer. So brother, I say it once and then put it away: You are the bravest warrior I know, and I thank you with my life."

Touch the Sky might have reminded Little Horse that, more than once, the sturdy young brave had placed his life on the line to save *him*, had stuck by him when very few others in the tribe besides Arrow Keeper or Honey Eater cared if he lived or died. But it was not the Cheyenne way to dwell on such things. Both youths knew, without words, that anyone who meant to kill one of them would have to kill both.

The camp had been reestablished well below the long ridge which separated them from the herd below. The buffalo were content to graze the lush bunchgrass of the river valley. The wind continued steadily to blow from the west, posing no threat of carrying their human smell to the buffalos and scattering the animals before the strike tomorrow.

Little Horse had killed a plump rabbit and dressed it out, and now they were building a fire to cook it. Touch the Sky, finally able to move without wincing at the pain, squatted to build a small bed of punk or dried, decayed wood. When it was finished he removed the flint and steel from the chamois pouch on his sash. A slicing blow with the steel against the small piece of flint sent a shower of sparks downward. The heat of the sparks soon caused some of the fine fibers of punk to smolder.

Carefully, Touch the Sky blew on the punk until he had coaxed it into flames. Then he piled on more substantial materials—dry wood shavings, fine splinters of wood, dry leaves and grass, then small sticks—to kindle a bigger fire.

"Word of what you did," Little Horse said, "has flown through the camp. Now there is much remorse over the beating you suffered. Even some of the Bull Whips who flogged you now say they did wrong. But when you whirl the water in the pool, you also stir up the mud. Your enemies are speaking against you. Keep your back to a tree."

Little Horse used the same arrow which had killed the rabbit as a spit, skewering it from throat to rump. He jabbed two forked sticks into the ground on both sides of the fire and placed the rabbit over the growing flames.

"Black Elk, Swift Canoe, and Wolf Who Hunts Smiling have put their heads together again. They are going among the Bull Whips, saying that once again you used white man's tactics, not the Cheyenne way. They tell all who will listen— and many still do—that you employ tricks learned from the blue-dressed soldiers who take our best hunting grounds.

"Just now, as I crossed camp, I heard Wolf Who Hunts Smiling speaking to his fawning admirers. 'Every time this make-believe Cheyenne earns the praise of the Headmen,' he told them, 'it is by some cunning piece of paleface trickery—where is the *Cheyenne* in him?' "

"All in good time," Touch the Sky said, "Wolf Who Hunts Smiling will die the dog's death he deserves. I am loathe to sully the Arrows by killing a Cheyenne. Only this has kept me from spilling his blood out onto the ground. But the reckoning is coming."

"Something is afoot," Little Horse said. "Count on it. They are determined to keep you from the hunt tomorrow."

Touch the Sky nodded. Later this night he would assist Arrow Keeper in the Renewal of the Sacred Arrows, an important rite before possible battle. And the "hidden eye" which Arrow Keeper was teaching him to develop as a shaman already told him there would be trouble during the ceremony.

Black Elk had noticed Honey Eater's sullen silence ever since she had arrived with the rest. He knew it was because she had seen the marks of the beating he and the other Bull Whips had inflicted on Touch the Sky.

Her silence infuriated him. What right did a squaw have to approve or disapprove of a war leader's actions? Though she was careful to avoid any open flaunting of her love for the tall youth, it was there for all to see.

Back at the permanent camp, he had passed the entrance of the women's sewing lodge and heard them at their song. And although it mentioned no names, it was clear enough whose love they sang about. Now the tribe was singing another song about Touch the Sky's bravery—as if no other warrior could violate Hunt Law and lead women and children around.

Now, as she served him a juicy hump steak on a thick piece of bark, he said, "I would speak with you."

Honey Eater had already turned away and started to leave. She stopped, waiting.

"Look at your husband!" he commanded her. "Your war leader is speaking!"

She finally turned, but kept her eyes cast downward.

"Honey Eater, I do not like your manner with me."

"What would you have of me?"

"I would have you remember that I am your husband!"

"Truly," she said bitterly, "I cannot forget this."

He suddenly threw the steak down on the ground. His breathing grew so fierce with anger that his nostrils flared.

"You will not take this tone with me! I could have had my pick of any woman in the tribe."

Honey Eater feared Black Elk's rage. But ever since seeing what he and the other Bull Whips had done to Touch the Sky, her own anger was deep and strong. Now she could not bite back her words as she usually did.

"Would that you had picked another! If you are not satisfied with the wife you have, you may sing the Throw-away Song and divorce me on the drum. *I* will shed no tears."

"No, you would not, for you are too eager to rut with your tall white man's dog! You call yourself a Cheyenne maiden? Where is your virtue, your modesty?"

"They are in the same place where you left behind your manly courage and fairness!"

Rage actually paralyzed him for a moment. "What do you mean by these words?" he demanded.

"I mean that I have seen what you, your hateful cousin Wolf Who Hunts Smiling, and the other 'courageous' Bull Whips have done to Touch the Sky."

"You she-bitch, hold your tongue! We have done what men will do when the Hunt Law must be upheld. I do not quarrel with women!

What right have you to question the actions of men?"

"I have eyes to see, ears to hear. And I do not think these were the actions of men, but the actions of cowards!"

This was incredible. Black Elk was so shocked at her insolence that he merely stared at her, his mouth gaping. The dancing firelight failed to soften his stern features, his fierce black eyes, the leathery hunk of dead ear he had sewn back on himself with buckskin thread after a Bluecoat saber had severed it in battle.

"You bitch in heat! You will not give your war leader a son, but you will pine away for *him,* a white man's dog who arrived among us wearing shoes and offering his hand to shake like the blue-bloused liars who shake our hands before they kill us! You *hope* that I will divorce you on the drum. But I swear by the sun, the moon, and the directions of the wind that I will take you out on the Plains if you do not learn to be a good Cheyenne wife!"

Now it was Honey Eater's turn to fill with hot rage. "Taking a woman out on the Plains" was the most severe punishment a Cheyenne man could inflict on a wife, and could not be done without clear proof that she had lain with another man. It had never, to her knowledge, been done in their tribe, though she had heard stories of it in other tribes. The man deserted his wife out in the wilderness and announced that she was available to any man in the tribe who wanted to rut on her. Though the woman was not banished, her shame afterward was so great that she was expected to kill herself. In reality, a man who did such a

129

thing, no matter for what cause, could never be respected again.

"You speak this way to me," she said, "and call yourself a warrior? I am the daughter of the great Chief Yellow Bear. I will not be threatened like this! You already went too far when you cut my braid. Do not forget that a Cheyenne woman too can petition the Star Chamber for a divorce."

But she had pushed Black Elk too far with these words. A moment later she cried out in shock when the powerful brave brought the side of his fist against her face hard, knocking her down.

"Place my words in your pockets," he told her in a cold, dangerously low voice. "I swear I will kill you *and* him before I let that false Cheyenne mount you! Do you have ears for this?"

But Honey Eater was beyond words now. She held her already swelling face, great sobs hitching in her chest.

"Prepare my clothing and war bonnet for the Medicine Arrows ceremony," he said. "And pray that your tall buck does not cross me, or I swear I will turn him into worm fodder!"

Chapter 13

The buffalo herd on their left flank provided a natural defense against any Kiowa-Comanche attack launched from that direction. Likewise, the Red River protected the northern approach, and a series of deep redrock canyons the southern approach.

The only vulnerable spot was their right flank, and Black Elk had already ordered a strong guard to protect it. The hunt would go on as planned tomorrow. But the hunters would be in constant communication with the sentries by way of signals flashed with fragments of mirrors. At the first sign of attack, they would rush back toward the camp and head it off before it reached the women and children and elders.

Touch the Sky belonged to no clan. But Arrow

Keeper, as always, had instructed the women of his Owl Clan to erect the young brave's tipi. The youth was crossing the central clearing, heading toward his tipi to prepare for the Medicine Arrows ceremony, when he spotted Honey Eater.

She carried her curved skinning knife, blood pail, and other equipment. He knew she was probably on her way to join the other women in her clan, making preparations for the skinning and butchering tomorrow after the kill. Fires had been kept to a minimum, and he couldn't tell if Black Elk was lurking nearby. Playing it safe, he started to veer wide around the girl.

A moment later, however, she passed close to the small fire under the cooking tripod outside Arrow Keeper's tipi. Though she turned her face hastily away, Touch the Sky spotted the nasty, swollen bruise covering nearly half of one side of her face.

Black Elk's handiwork! The jealous, hotheaded warrior had beaten her.

Touch the Sky's anger was sudden and deep. For a moment he almost ran after her to catch her and question her. But he decided against this—there was no question as to what had happened.

The only question now, he told himself, is what am I going to do about it?

He had warned Black Elk before to keep his hands off her. Warnings had clearly had no effect. Now it was time to give up on words and do as Black Elk himself often preached—let deeds speak for words.

He went to Black Elk's tipi and found the war leader seated before the entrance flap, sharpening his knife on a whetstone.

Comanche Raid

Keeping all emotion out of his voice, Touch the Sky said, "Black Elk, I would speak with you."

Black Elk glanced up at him, immediately wary. "I have nothing to say to you, make-believe Cheyenne."

"No," Touch the Sky agreed, "I have something to say to you."

"Whatever it may be, I have no ears for it."

"If you value life itself, you will find ears for it."

Black Elk scowled. "Do you threaten me?"

"I have had done with threats. Now, I swear by Maiyun, you will listen! You and your worthless cousin call me a white man's dog until I am weary of hearing it. Then so it is. This white man's dog *did* learn some tricks from the hair faces, Black Elk. Let me teach you one of them."

Without another word, Touch the Sky reached down and plucked the warrior's bone-handle knife from his hand and threw it into the surrounding bushes.

For a long moment Black Elk's face looked as surprised as it had when Honey Eater called him a coward. Then, suddenly, he was on his feet.

"Clearly," he said, "you are looking for your own grave."

"Not at all," Touch the Sky said. "I am here to show you what I learned from the palefaces. See, now you stand without a weapon to hand. Let me show you a trick."

A heartbeat later he delivered a powerful upper-cut to the point of Black Elk's chin. It was a smashing right fist, exactly like the blow which Hiram Steele's wrangler Boone Wilson had given Touch the Sky when the Cheyenne was caught with Steele's daughter Kristen.

Black Elk staggered back hard, almost falling.

Touch the Sky waded in quickly before the brave could recover his balance.

"See, Black Elk? This is how white dogs are taught to fight—with their paws curled into fists. Here is some more."

He brought a hard right to Black Elk's stomach, a left jab to the war leader's face. The blows were powerful, backed by hard muscle and deep wrath. Black Elk, like most Indians, knew little of boxing. Without a weapon, all he knew to do was wrestle. But the quick flurry of blows had left him stunned.

"How do you like it, Panther Clan? Now you know what it is like for Honey Eater when you strike her."

A final hard right to the jaw dropped Black Elk where he stood.

"Now you *will* have ears for my words," Touch the Sky said.

He removed his own knife from its beaded sheath and suddenly slashed his own inner left arm, drawing a scarlet ribbon of blood to trail into the ground at Black Elk's feet.

"Now I make this blood vow, Black Elk. The next time I see or learn of you hurting her, I swear by the sun and the earth that I live on you *will* die a hard death! I will send you under and sully the Sacred Arrows. I do not care if it means my banishment. I am alone anyway, thanks to you and your cousin."

Black Elk was too stunned to get back up immediately. But as Touch the Sky started to walk away, he called out.

"You might as well sing the death song now, White Man's Shoes! Everyone in the tribe knows that you long to put on the old moccasin." To a Cheyenne, "putting on the old moccasin" was a reference to a single man who wanted to marry a one-time married woman. "But you will have to kill me first!"

Touch the Sky turned back around.

"All in good time, Dead Ear. I have glanced the other way when you tried to murder me. When you played the white-livered coward and sent your cousin and Swift Canoe to kill me at Medicine Lake. When you fired at an 'elk' that turned out to be me instead. I am done trying to make peace with low-crawling cowards who speak in a wolf bark and beat women.

"I say it again, and you had best place these words next to your heart. Hurt Honey Eater one more time and this white man's dog will feed your liver to the carrion birds."

While Touch the Sky was setting Black Elk on the ground, Wolf Who Hunts Smiling was up to his own tricks.

The young warrior was extremely ambitious and harbored secret dreams of someday leading the Cheyenne Nation in a war of extermination against the whites. Like most Indians, he had no actual concept of their numbers. But his hatred for white men had festered inside him like a poisonous canker ever since he had stood by, horrified, when blue-bloused soldiers turned his father into stew meat with a double charge of canister shot. And this Touch the Sky, had he not lived

135

among the paleface devils so long that he permanently carried their stink?

He was also a serious obstacle to his plans. Clearly, old Arrow Keeper, perhaps the most respected elder among all the Shayiena people, favored the pretend Cheyenne. Selecting him to train as a shaman was a great honor. A tribal medicine man, in his own way, could wield as much power and influence as a chief—even more, since the Cheyenne faith in the supernatural was strong.

Wolf Who Hunts Smiling was no fool. He had seen how strong his people's faith in visions and medicine dreams was. And he also knew that this Touch the Sky supposedly possessed the gift of visions. He was not sure how much he himself believed in visions, but he was certain that Touch the Sky was a liar. Clearly, the white man's dog was cleverly pretending to walk the Spirit Path. He knew full well that Arrow Keeper, who had begun to dote and drool in his frosted years, and some of the others would be impressed.

So now it was time to trap the fox in his own den.

With Swift Canoe at his side, he was paying a secret visit to an old squaw named Calf Woman of the Root Eaters Clan. Calf Woman had at least 70 winters behind her and was generally considered to be a soft-brain. However, it was common knowledge that visions were often received by the sick, dying, and mentally infirm. And Calf Woman had a certain reputation for pronouncing visions which had come true.

She also had a reputation for her love of white man's coffee and sugar. And in his legging sash

Wolf Who Hunts Smiling carried a little of both. He and Swift Canoe had obtained these at the trading post in Red Shale in exchange for pelts and furs.

Fortunately, it was dark around her tipi and no one would see them paying this visit. The two youths found the old woman sitting before the raised entrance flap, sipping yarrow tea from a buffalo-horn cup.

"Good evening, Grandmother," Wolf Who Hunts Smiling greeted her respectfully.

She peered up curiously at the two new arrivals, trying to make out their faces in the grainy twilight.

"Is that you, Half Bear?"

Swift Canoe dug an elbow into Wolf Who Hunts Smiling's ribs. Half Bear was the old woman's son, but he had died many winters ago during the battle with the Pawnee at Beaver Creek.

"Brother," Swift Canoe whispered, "this old hag has been struck by lightning. Best to leave it alone."

Wolf Who Hunts Smiling shook him off and said patiently, "No, Grandmother. It is Wolf Who Hunts Smiling of the Panther Clan and Swift Canoe of the Wolverine Clan. We have come to see how you are getting along."

The old woman vaguely recognized the clan names and their faces. But both names were unknown to her addled brain. Still, it was a fine thing for such young men to come visit an old woman like this. She smiled her toothless smile and bade them sit down beside her.

"Here, Grandmother," Wolf Who Hunts Smiling said, "let me put some sugar in your tea."

"Sugar?"

"Yes, Grandmother, not honey. Fine white man's sugar."

The old woman gripped her cup eagerly with both hands and drank the tea down quickly. She smacked her lips together appreciatively, glancing with longing at the drawstring pouch in the boy's hand. Purposely, Wolf Who Hunts Smiling dangled it as he spoke.

"I have heard a thing, Grandmother. I have heard that you are blessed with visions."

She nodded, still watching the pouch. "Sometimes Maiyun opens the hidden eye for me, yes."

"What sorts of things do you then see, old one?"

At a sign from Wolf Who Hunts Smiling, Swift Canoe stirred up the dying embers of the old woman's fire. Now they could see the deep lines and crags of her face, the scrawny shoulders hunched under her red blanket.

Swift Canoe dumped the last of the tea out of her baked-clay kettle and added more water from the bladder bag nearby. He threw a little coffee in to boil. Despite her advanced age, Calf Woman smelled it instantly.

"Is that coffee?" she asked eagerly.

"Yes, indeed," Wolf Who Hunts Smiling said. "Fine white man's coffee, not the bitter brew which our Southern kin acquire from the Mexicans. It will be very tasty with sugar in it."

"May I have some?"

"Have some? Grandmother, we are preparing it for you."

She smiled happily. Wolf Who Hunts Smiling repeated his question. "What do you see in your visions, Grandmother?"

Comanche Raid

"I see many things, child. I have seen revelations, and I have seen curses. When War Bonnet was killed by Pawnees, I saw it happen while he still lay sleeping in his tipi. When Sun Road lost the sacred Medicine Hat, a vision told me where to find it."

The coffee was boiling now, the deep, rich aroma wafting into the old woman's nostrils.

"These are fine things indeed," Wolf Who Hunts Smiling said. He handed the horn cup to Swift Canoe, who poured some coffee into it. Wolf Who Hunts Smiling added a few generous pinches of sugar and handed it to Calf Woman.

She sipped at it. "*Ipewa*," she said in Cheyenne. "Good."

"Tell me, Grandmother," Wolf Who Hunts Smiling said. "Have you never had a vision concerning this Touch the Sky?"

She glanced up from the cup. "Touch the Sky?"

"The tall youth who arrived in our camp four winters ago dressed in white man's clothing?"

She shook her head. "I think not."

"Are you sure, Grandmother?" Wolf Who Hunts Smiling added another pinch of sugar to her coffee. His furtive eyes never left the old woman. "Perhaps if you could recall a vision about him, there would be more coffee and sugar in it for you."

"More coffee and sugar?"

"All of this," Wolf Who Hunts Smiling assured the confused old woman, proffering the packets.

The old woman stared at them covetously. Coffee and sugar were fine things indeed. And truly, she had had many visions in her time.

"Perhaps," Wolf Who Hunts Smiling suggested,

reading the look on her face, "you have simply forgotten it?"

"Perhaps," she agreed.

Wolf Who Hunts Smiling shared a victorious glance with Swift Canoe.

"Let us see," the youth said, tucking the coffee and sugar into her sash, "if we can refresh your memory."

Chapter 14

Soon after Wolf Who Hunts Smiling and Swift Canoe visited old Calf Woman, the Renewal of the Medicine Arrows ceremony was held. Once again Touch the Sky would serve as assistant to Arrow Keeper.

The entire tribe began to gather in the middle of their temporary camp, although this time only the warriors would actually participate in leaving gifts for the Arrows. The Renewal was held annually, and before battle, and after some serious crime such as murder had sullied the entire people.

The Kiowa and Comanche had no taboo against attacking by night. So all the warriors had their battle rigs ready and to hand. Women and older children had all armed themselves with knives,

141

clubs, and spiked tomahawks. Sentries had been posted, and would be relieved later to make their sacrifices to the Arrows.

Touch the Sky donned his mountain lion skin, again wondering for a moment—had its big medicine protected him from bullets and arrows during the attack on the hunt camp, or had he just been fortunate? He braided his long, loose locks and then wrapped them with strips of red-painted buckskin.

Two Twists and the other junior warriors were especially proud. As recognition of their bravery during the attack, they would be participating in the Renewal for the first time. Tomorrow, during the hunt, they would serve as the all-important guard on the tribe's vulnerable east flank—in the direction of the rising sun, out of which the Kiowa and Comanche often chose to attack.

For a moment, before he left his tipi and joined the gathering clans, Touch the Sky stared off into the darkness which surrounded the camp.

He heard nothing to cause fear: only the occasional bellowing of a buffalo bull in the nearby valley, or the staccato barking of coyotes. But although the sentries had not raised the wolf howl of alarm, he sensed the presence of their enemy nearby.

Nor were all his enemies outside the clan circles. Again he heard Little Horse's warning: *Keep your back to a tree.*

His beating of Black Elk earlier had marked a new stage in their mutual hatred. For the first time he had gone on the offensive and whipped his enemy into temporary submission. But he knew Black Elk would never brook such treatment. And Wolf Who Hunts Smiling had been convinced, after the Bull Whips flogged him during the hunt, that Touch the Sky would again be clearly marked as an outsider. He had been seething ever since his enemy's rescue of the noncombatants had again restored Touch the Sky to a position of some respect in the eyes of the others.

However, there was no time now to dwell on such thoughts. He heard the rhythmic drumming start as young women began the dance beat, pounding on hollow logs and shaking gourds filled with pebbles.

Many had gathered by the time he joined Arrow Keeper in front of a cottonwood stump. A huge ceremonial fire illuminated the clearing and the coyote-fur pouch atop the stump, which held the four sacred Medicine Arrows that symbolized the fate of the tribe.

Touch the Sky spotted Black Elk in his best war bonnet, coup feathers trailing the ground behind him. Many stared curiously at the dark bruises discoloring his face, knowing full well how he must have gotten them.

But when Honey Eater stepped into the firelight, Touch the Sky had eyes for no one else. Indeed, everyone in the tribe stared in awe.

She had never looked this beautiful. She wore her finest doeskin dress with a tasseled belt of buffalo hair. The dress was adorned with dyed elk teeth, gold coins, brightly dyed feathers. She had donned new quilled moccasins and her finest bone choker. No attempt had been made to disguise her mutilated hair. It was as if she wore

Black Elk's unjust punishment as a badge of honor.

Touch the Sky also spotted Wolf Who Hunts Smiling and Swift Canoe when they exchanged conspiratorial glances. Some new trouble was in the wind, and Touch the Sky expected it to blow his way.

Arrow Keeper opened the ceremony with a prayer of praise and thanks to Maiyun, the Great Medicine Man. Then, one after another, the painted warriors began dancing around the fire, kicking their knees high and shouting *"Hi-ya, hi-ya!"* over and over in time to the pounding rhythms. Since a possible battle loomed, they would fast from now until the danger was over. Although this sometimes weakened them, it also created the lightheaded trance which encouraged brave deeds—and immunity to pain—in battle.

At a signal from Arrow Keeper, Touch the Sky stepped behind the stump. He scattered rich tobacco as an offering to the four directions, the sun, and the moon. Then, his face solemn with pride, he carefully unwrapped the four Sacred Arrows.

An absolute hush fell over the entire gathering. Not even a child coughed. One by one, the noncombatants filed by for a rare peek at the prize which old Arrow Keeper had sworn to protect with his life. Touch the Sky had lain two of them horizontally, the other two across them vertically. They were striped in bright blue and yellow, tipped with chipped stone, fletched with scarlet-dyed feathers.

After the rest had glimpsed the Arrows which must be kept forever sweet and clean, Arrow

Comanche Raid

Keeper called out to the warriors to offer their gifts to the Arrows.

Valuable items were soon heaped before the stump as, one by one, the braves filed by: new bows, a handsome parfleche with intricate beadwork, a fine tow wallet, enemy scalps, wool blankets, clay pipes, brand-new moccasins and leggings, a lace shawl, a leather shirt, a foxskin quiver, an obsidian knife with moonstones laid into its bone handle. It cost Touch the Sky extra effort not to smile when Two Twists and the warriors-in-training filed by last, their faces sternly proud at this important rite of passage to manhood.

When the last gift was piled on the heap, Arrow Keeper declared the Arrows renewed and chanted the closing prayer. But before the people could scatter to their clan circles, old Calf Woman boldly stepped into the flickering circle of the firelight and made a startling announcement.

"Hear an old woman's words! I have had an important vision concerning the tribe."

The first reaction was one of collective shock. Cheyenne women never put themselves forward in tribal ceremonies. But a vision was an important thing, and Calf Woman was said to possess the gift of visions.

Everyone, including Chief Gray Thunder, looked to Arrow Keeper.

"Speak this thing you have seen," Arrow Keeper told her.

"There is to be a battle soon," she said. "Very soon, before the hunt is over. We have just renewed the Arrows. So, it is good. But in my vision, there was blood on the Sacred Arrows."

A low murmur erupted. Blood on the Arrows meant blood on the tribe. Much blood.

"This blood," she continued, "was caused by a reckless youth who violated the sacred Hunt Law. The Great Medicine Man is angry, the buffalo are angry. The generous gifts of Maiyun were carelessly squandered when buffalo were sent over a cliff to die. Now many, many Cheyenne people must die to atone—not just our warriors, but our women and children and the old ones."

Her words struck Touch the Sky with the force of a battle lance. Every head turned to stare at him. Warm blood crept up the back of his neck and into his face. He knew Calf Woman on sight, of course, but had never spoken to her—though her Root Eaters Clan was well respected. Clearly, however, she could be talking of no one else but him.

Arrow Keeper was troubled. Frowning, he said, "Calf Woman, are you sure this thing was a vision and not just *odjib*, a thing of smoke? You have seen many winters, and sometimes a weary mind may confuse a dream in the little day with the Spirit Path."

"It was a medicine dream, shaman," she insisted, "not a dream in the little day. It came upon me in full waking hours, all at once, and was over in a heartbeat."

This testimony drew more troubled murmuring from the others. Indeed, this was the way visions came unless they were deliberately sought.

Now Chief Gray Thunder interceded.

"Old Grandmother, I was there at Beaver Creek when your son Half Bear fell to a Pawnee battle-ax. Long now have you served the tribe and taught our young women the beadwork which makes our tribe the envy of the Plains. You are a good woman. But in the hoary years, a mind may slip its tether occasionally. Are you sure of this thing?"

"I am sure, Gray Thunder. And as penance for this violation of Hunt Law, Maiyun told me, the errant youth must set up a pole to ward off this disaster."

More talk erupted from the people. Chief Gray Thunder folded his arms until all had quieted. "Setting up a pole" was a harsh voluntary penance which could expiate a sin against the Arrows. It could not be ordered; the transgressor must agree on his own to do it. The grueling ordeal consisted of setting up a pole on a hill and hanging from it for the better part of a day by bone hooks driven through the chest muscles.

Now Arrow Keeper was deeply troubled. The Cheyenne faith in vision compulsion was deep and strong. He knew that this faith was sometimes abused—murderers had avoided banishment, for example, by claiming that Maiyun ordered them in a vision to kill.

On the other hand, the law of the Vision Way was clear: If Maiyun did truly speak to a mortal in a vision, His voice could not be ignored. The price for ignoring his command was death or insanity. And in this case, an entire tribe was being compelled to an action—failure to do as told might thus mean the destruction of the entire tribe.

Arrow Keeper was fully aware of the deceit Touch the Sky's enemies were capable of. This might well be a ruse, and the youth had already suffered greatly from the unjust whipping. But was it worth risking the entire tribe to find out if the old grandmother spoke straight-arrow?

"Fathers! Brothers!" Little Horse said. "This thing would be scanned! I too respect Calf Woman and her clan. But the frosted years are upon her, and this time I do not believe she has truth firmly by the tail!"

"You *would* speak up for your friend," Black Elk said, "no matter what the outcome for your tribe. When he left his tribe to fight for the whites, you went with him then too, though we were surrounded by enemies and needed every warrior."

Many of the Bull Whips spoke up in support of Black Elk's words.

"Like Little Horse I too am troubled by this," said Spotted Tail, leader of the Bowstrings. "Touch the Sky was soundly whipped for his misadventure with the buffalo. Why would Maiyun demand such a harsh additional punishment as this?"

Some others spoke out in favor of this. Again Gray Thunder folded his arms until it grew quiet. Honey Eater, her face tense, listened to the proceedings with her lower lip caught between her teeth. Black Elk saw this and scowled darkly.

"It is not our place to question the decisions of the Supernatural," he put in. "We mortals debate in council, and this is a good thing, But the pronouncements of Maiyun are not for debate. They are meant to be carried out. All of you here know well the price to be paid for ignoring His will."

Even Arrow Keeper had to agree Black Elk had spoken well this time. This was a terrible dilemma, pitting the welfare of the tribe against the suffering of a youth who had already been far more wronged than any other in the tribe.

Touch the Sky, for his part, had already realized everything as old Arrow Keeper had. Now, as every face in camp turned toward him—some sympathetic, some accusing, others simply confused—he realized how cleverly Wolf Who Hunts Smiling and Swift Canoe had trapped him. He could not be forced to this terrible, painful ordeal which had been known to kill a man. But if he refused, once again he would seem to put his own life ahead of the tribe's.

"Enough!" he said, his voice clear and strong. "Calf Woman claims she had a vision. Though I suspect this 'vision' was placed over her eyes by hands other than Maiyun's, I cannot call a respected old grandmother a liar. She claims I must set up a pole or our people are lost. So let all debate end and the tribe retire to their tipis. Tomorrow, I will swing from the pole!"

Earlier, Stone Mountain and Kicking Bird had slipped past the Cheyenne sentries by way of the river. The scouts pulled their frail boat, made of buffalo hides stretched across a frame of green cottonwood, up onto the sandy bank just below the enemy camp. Walking on their heels to avoid leaving footprints, they stashed it in a thicket and crept right up on the camp.

Kicking Bird had once been a prisoner of the Southern Cheyennes for several moons and understood much of their tongue. Soon he had learned of their plans for tomorrow. He Bear's Kiowa Apache had joined the combined Kiowa-Comanche band earlier. Now the attack was set.

They had learned all they needed to know. Now it was time to return to their people and report. But Kicking Bird lingered some moments longer, admiring the beautiful Cheyenne girl with the harshly cropped hair.

They must be sure to grab this one; she would fetch a good price. Even the ragged hair could not detract from her finely sculpted cheekbones, huge, almond-shaped eyes, flawless skin like wild honey. The doeskin dress clung to the sweeping curves of her hips like a second skin. She was surely much finer to look at than the venereal-tainted Mandan women he had known from many raids in the north country.

And now here was another piece of good luck. The brazen young buck who had ruined their earlier attack on the first camp would be alone and helpless while the rest were hunting.

The Comanche smiled to himself in the darkness. Soon he would no longer have to suck the tar out of his pipe; there would be plenty of tobacco once the Comancheros in Santa Fe paid for a fine group of Cheyenne slaves. And this tall brave who had stood boldly before the attack—those hooks through his breasts would seem like child's play compared to what the Red Raiders of the Plains had in store for him.

Chapter 15

Hairy Wolf used a pointed stick to draw a diagram in the dirt. Iron Eyes and He Bear, the newly arrived Kiowa Apache war leader who had led 20 seasoned braves to join this fight, crouched on both sides of him.

They were hidden in a wide apron of shade behind a mesa to the east of their enemy's camp. The warriors of all three tribes huddled behind them in small groups, checking their weapons for the final time and passing around earthen jars of *pulque* or cactus liquor. None of the warriors in this group, unlike their enemies from the Northern Plains, was worrying about counting first coup or undergoing elaborate religious rites. Southern Plains tribes did not count coup nor care as much about scalping. War was not for honor, but for goods and profit.

Neither did they harbor taboos about attacking at night. But He Bear had not arrived until well after dawn with his warriors, and their numbers without his band were not great enough against the well-armed Cheyenne—fanatical warriors who did not retreat until they or their enemy were dead. Nor would they be able to engage in their favorite attack tactic, circling in an ever-tightening pattern. The land around here would not permit it, nor the scattered line of hunters.

"South of the herd and the Cheyenne camp," Hairy Wolf said, drawing a ragged trench, "are the redrock canyons. The tribe has these canyons to its left flank, the herd dead ahead, the river on its right flank. They must ride straight into our main force, which I will lead."

"This has a good look to it," He Bear agreed. "*Me gusta*. Trapping them is a good thing, and so is attacking them like the paleface soldiers like to attack. These Cheyenne dogs, they like to flee on their ponies until the pursuers' horses tire. Then they whirl and suddenly attack. This way, they have no room for such tricks."

"Even better," Hairy Wolf said, "Iron Eyes will lead a hidden force of his Comanches on their most surefooted ponies. He knows a secret trail once used by the Navajos. It leads deep through the redrock canyons to the south. He will approach unseen through the canyons while my force attacks head-on."

"My warriors slip up from the canyons," Iron Eyes said. "They stay carefully behind the hunters as they desert the hunt and turn back to rush out past the camp and meet Hairy Wolf's force.

We can grab all the slaves we can carry, without once getting off our mounts," he added boastfully. "They will realize soon enough, but these are our fastest ponies. None of theirs will catch ours in this country we know much better than they. Once we reach the Llano, they won't have a chance."

"What about this young shaman?" He Bear said. Unlike the Kiowa, who left their long hair unrestrained, He Bear and his warriors wore red flannel bands. "You say he remained unscathed by bullets or arrows during your first attack. And the Pawnees refused to attack the Cheyenne Chief Renewal ceremony one spring after this one supposedly commanded a grizzly to attack them. I'd like to see such a big Indian."

"Before they join Iron Eyes and the rest, Red Sleeves and Standing Feather will pay him a visit while he swings from the pole, another of their superstitious practices. They will slice off his eyelids and slit his belly enough to pull some gut through for the carrion birds. He fancies himself defiant, but watching the crows eat his entrails will make him beg like the rest who defy us."

Before the hunters rode out for the kill next day, the Bull Whip soldiers took charge of Touch the Sky's punishment.

As the custom for voluntary penance required, Touch the Sky selected his own sturdy cottonwood limb and sliced it from the tree with an ax. He spiked one end, then followed Lone Bear and the rest of the Bull Whip troop to a lone hill just south of camp. From there, everyone who stayed behind could watch him swing all day. And the hunters would all see him as they filed by.

Touch the Sky held his mouth in its grim, determined slit. Again the punishment was unjust, but how could he prove he did not have the stink on him and was not frightening off the buffalo? Calf Woman's "vision" had not convinced everyone in the tribe, true. But enough were impressed by the realization that the entire tribe might be suffering because of him—and indeed, in his confused heart of hearts, Touch the Sky thought it possible that he did carry the stink.

So he never once hesitated as he secured one end of the pole into the dirt at the top of the hill. Nor did he flinch when Lone Bear drew the curved-bone hooks out of the parfleche over his hip.

"Remember this," Lone Bear said, "I did not declare this punishment. You chose it, buck. Now it must go forward. I will see that the thing is done right."

"I see clear enough," Touch the Sky said, "that Wolf Who Hunts Smiling and Black Elk are keen for this."

"They may be, but *I* am not!" a Bull Whip said, though a stone-eyed glance from Lone Bear hushed him.

Another brave tied Touch the Sky's hands behind him with sturdy rawhide thongs looped tight over both wrists. The same tough rawhide was used for the halter arrangement which was attached to the hooks and would fit over the top of the pole. From this he would dangle, his weight held by hooks in his muscles.

Without another word, Lone Bear drove the first hook deep into the hard-sloping curve of

Touch the Sky's left pectoral muscle. There was surprisingly little blood, but the pain corded his neck and arched his entire body like a bow.

He met first Black Elk's, then Wolf Who Hunts Smiling's eyes and held them, showing them no fear or pain—only hatred and the promise of sure vengeance. Then his vision blurred when Lone Bear drove in the second finely honed hook.

But that pain was as nothing compared to the sensation when several braves picked him up and lashed the halter to the pole. His feet dangled only a short distance above the ground. But it was enough to leave all his body weight tugging on the hooks. They felt like giant rattlesnake fangs trying to pierce through to his heart.

"You will hang there until the last buffalo is killed today," Lone Bear said. "This is decreed by Hunt Law. Any who attempts to help you will hang beside you."

But Touch the Sky, deep lance-points of pain ripping through him, held his mouth slitted and refused to make a sound.

Long after the hunters had ridden out, Arrow Keeper stood beyond the last clan circle of conical tipis. He stared toward the grotesque sight on the hill above him, his heart stung with pain for the youth's suffering.

How viciously clever his enemies had been this time! There was no way out for Touch the Sky. Had he refused this penance, every bit of bad luck from now on would be blamed on him. And truly, the tribe was not short on bad luck and suffering.

All of this had been foretold in Arrow Keeper's first great vision, the same vision Touch the Sky had eventually sought for himself. The hand of the Supernatural was in this thing. But so too were many trials and sufferings for the youth once called Matthew Hanchon—a name for which he had paid dearly ever since leaving the white man's world for the red man's.

Too dearly, Arrow Keeper suddenly decided.

Watching the young buck hang out there, the skin of his breasts stretched to the point of tearing, he made up his mind to visit old Calf Woman.

The pain was too great, too intensely focused in his chest, for Touch the Sky to put it completely outside of himself. He hung semiconscious now, the morning sun growing hotter on his stinging flesh. His vision alternated between blurry awareness of his surroundings and a red film of pain as effective as a blindfold.

He had been aware, earlier, when a rumbling thunder and the angry bellowing of bulls announced that the herd had begun to stampede. It was followed by the sharp cries of the hunters as they gave pursuit, beginning to isolate sections of the herd. But he knew it would be a long time before the final kill was complete and someone returned to free him.

When he saw the two Comanche braves climb over the rim of the nearby canyon, headed straight for him, he realized his tribe's mistake in ignoring the rugged string of canyons.

One of them removed a knife from its beaded sheath. Touch the Sky could not even lash out at them with his feet as they came closer—the slightest motion sent additional fiery pain throbbing deep into his chest.

The war-painted Comanche raised the narrow-bladed knife toward Touch the Sky's left eye and brought the tip against the soft skin where the eyelid met the forehead. The Cheyenne knew he meant to remove the lids and leave his eyes to literally bake in the glaring sun.

The next moment a rifle spoke its piece, and a gout of blood and brain erupted from the knife-wielding Comanche's skull. A heartbeat later, a throwing ax split open the rib cage of the second one.

And then there was another moment of intense pain, a flash of red, filmy confusion before Touch the Sky briefly passed out. When he came to again, he was lying in mercifully cool grass. Arrow Keeper, young Two Twists, and another of the junior warriors leaned anxiously over him.

"When I found Calf Woman boiling coffee," Arrow Keeper told his young apprentice, "it was easy enough to learn from her that Wolf Who Hunts Smiling and Swift Canoe had been playing the foxes. They will pay for this, little brother. I have already sent a runner ahead to the hunt, commanding the soldiers to arrest them. I went to Gray Thunder. It was he who issued this order to free you immediately."

Wincing, but forcing himself to sit up, Touch the Sky said, "Father, do not arrest Wolf Who Hunts Smiling yet! He is too good a fighter, and warriors will be needed. Those two Comanches came up out of the canyons. I fear our enemies have used them for some graver purpose too."

*   *   *

When the mirror signal was flashed by one of the Comanches down in the canyon, Hairy Wolf's main band launched a direct attack on the Cheyenne camp.

Cries of "Remember Wolf Creek!" echoed through the riders as their well-trained mounts raised spiraling whirlwinds of alkali dust. As intended, they were almost immediately spotted by the Cheyenne sentries. They, in turn, flashed signals to the warriors engaged in the hunt, urgently summoning them back.

Below in the canyon, Iron Eyes had decided on the added precaution of dividing his braves into two groups. They would ride up separately and approach the camp behind the hunters from two different directions. Once the battle had begun forward of camp, they would strike quickly while the foolish Cheyenne were preoccupied in counting coup.

Touch the Sky heard the first wolf howls of alarm from the junior warriors even as he was returning to camp, Arrow Keeper and Two Twists helping him walk.

Now they could hear the attacking enemy as they approached, see the swirling dust on the horizon to the east. Soon the main body of Cheyenne hunters rode hard from the west to meet the fight before it could reach the camp.

As Little Horse flashed by, long, loose black locks streaming in the wind, Touch the Sky desperately signaled him to stop. At the same moment he stopped young Two Twists as the youth prepared to mount and join the defending force.

"We must ride back toward the herd," he shouted to his friends above the din of the riders. "I fear the slave-takers have cleverly tricked us by using the canyons! This attack to the east, it is a diversion!"

He nearly cried out at the protesting pain in his chest when he swung up onto his gray and pushed her hard to the west, toward the river valley and the now-stampeding herd. But his suspicions were soon confirmed: All three Cheyennes saw it when a score of well-armed braves streamed up out of the canyon ahead of them, heading east toward the camp.

Touch the Sky made only one fatal mistake: He assumed this was the entire force. In fact it was only half of Iron Eyes' men.

His mind was preoccupied with a greater problem: As the sounds of a fierce battle rose behind them, where the two main forces were closing for the kill, he had to decide how three Cheyennes were going to stop 20 braves from reaching the women and children.

One possible answer came to him when he saw the band maneuver itself between a sharp cliff and the last fragment of the panicked buffalo herd. Truly, the Cheyenne were too few to stop the slave-takers—but perhaps a few hundred charging buffalo could literally send them under.

He desperately signaled his companions and they nodded agreement. They fired their rifles, whistled, and shouted their shrill war cry to turn the buffalo. The furious bulls constantly tried to gore his pony as Touch the Sky recklessly, desperately pushed the gray right up tight against them.

Realizing the Comanches were about to burst out into the open, Touch the Sky made a final, dangerous effort. Linked to his pony only by a handful of mane, he swung his entire body free and lashed out hard with both feet full into the bearded face of the biggest bull.

After the hard impact, his legs flew down into the unbroken sea of shaggy fur and he felt himself trapped tight between two of the animals. Then, even as the momentarily intimidated bull veered sharply toward the cliff, Touch the Sky made a supreme effort to outwrestle death and won—he wrenched his upper body hard, and a moment later he was bouncing freely on the back of his pony.

The buffalo barely avoided the cliff as they swerved. Nearly half of Iron Eyes' band were not so lucky. The inexorable weight of the herd literally swept them, screaming, over the edge to a hard death on the flint and rock rubble below. This unnerved the others, who turned and fled back into the canyon on foot when their ponies panicked, several of them leaping over the cliff to death.

Touch the Sky, Little Horse, and Two Twists all raised high their lances in victory. But there was no time to celebrate now. As one, they let out their war cry and raced to join the main battle east of camp.

From the canyon brim, Iron Eyes and the remaining force of 20 had watched once again as the young medicine man defeated sure death and routed their companions. But clearly he was not infallible—look now how he rode to join the feint! These Northerners had a good deal to learn about the art of war as fought by those who had driven out the Spaniards.

He had just shed good Comanche blood. Now his tribe would pay dearly. Scalps were worthless things, good only for a bit of decoration in a war lodge. It was the *living* who were valuable. The Northern tribes were averse to slave-taking, but why? What more logical way to literally profit from revenge?

And the Cheyenne women, were they not the best and the cleanest on the Plains? Until marriage they wore a knotted-rope chastity belt, and any man who touched that belt would never smoke the common pipe again. With the dripping diseases so common, they brought top prices from the Comancheros who delivered them to their new owners.

Iron Eyes had heard the scouts speaking about this slender maiden with the cropped hair—how she was as proud as she was beautiful. The Comancheros would not miss a few bites off of a juicy steak. Before she was sold, the Comanche men would teach this beauty about pride.

Chapter 16

The battle turned out to be less fierce than it sounded.

At first Touch the Sky rejoiced when he saw the attackers fighting a retreating battle. Most of the gunshots he, Little Horse, and Two Twists had heard were from Comanche pistols. Though good Colt cavalry guns, ideal for close combat, they were ineffective at longer ranges. The Comanches were used to firing them just to make noise, in the same way that they again sounded their captured Bluecoat bugle. And like most Southern Plains tribes they were spendthrifts with ammunition. The next raid would always provide.

The Cheyennes, however, along with their cousins the Sioux, had learned bitter lessons from the blue-dressed palefaces about conserving ammunition and powder. They were also much better equipped this year with rifles. Many of the enemy's bullets and arrows had fallen short, and the attackers did not seem keen for combat with knives and battle-axes—though once an agile Comanche brave turned around to face a Cheyenne pursuer and managed to stun his pony with a vicious blow of his stone skull-cracker.

Despite the Comanche superiority on horseback, the Cheyennes had developed an evasive riding style which impressed their enemy. When within range of enemy bullets, they clung by their feet to the pony's neck, then tucked their body down so that the enemy saw only their feet and occasionally a face glimpsing at them from under the pony's head. They could even shoot accurately from this position, a fact which a taunting Kiowa soon discovered when he flew dead from his horse.

But overall, Touch the Sky noticed, the combined bands were content to lead their pursuers and avoid any battlefield heroics. It began to look more and more like a feint, not a battle. They were being drawn further and further east, away from camp.

Away from camp!

Trade rifles cracked from behind them, the plain but sturdy British guns favored by the Indians of Gray Thunder's tribe. Touch the Sky's eyes met Little Horse's. In that horrible moment, both braves suddenly realized their mistake.

When they whirled their ponies back toward camp, Two Twists joined them. Spotted Tail, Tangle Hair, and a few other Bowstrings had also heard the shots, and now the small band raced west in a skirmish line, the red streamers of their lances flying straight out in the wind.

More rifles cracked from the direction of camp; they could hear the shrill cries of the marauders even above the pounding of their galloping ponies. But all Touch the Sky could do was remember Honey Eater from the night of the Arrow Renewal, when she had looked so regally beautiful in her finery—so beautiful that even her stubbed hair could not mar her perfection.

Now he realized he had made a fatal mistake in judgment—that first band rising out of the canyon had not been the entire second force of warriors. He had shown further bad judgment when he led his friends in joining this sham attack instead of remaining at the camp.

This time he could not blame Black Elk or Wolf Who Hunts Smiling or any of his enemies. His carelessness had placed Honey Eater and the rest in danger too terrible to comprehend.

Desperately he dug his heels harder and harder into his pony's flanks. The shots from camp were less frequent now. But the first scream of a Cheyenne woman reached Touch the Sky's ears, and he cried out to Maiyun to *please* give them just a little more time.

Arrow Keeper too had watched the main battle turn into a rout by the Cheyenne braves. This was clearly not going to be another bloody Wolf Creek battle. But he knew better than to rejoice too early. His vision had clearly shown blood on the Arrows—not the literal blood of battle perhaps, but possibly a symbol of great suffering and loss for the tribe.

Comanche Raid

He had watched Touch the Sky fly past with the others to join the battle. Chief Gray Thunder too had ridden in the fight, though the Headmen would not let him leave the last line of riders. Arrow Keeper was accompanied by the elders, the women, and the children. Sure the tribe was momentarily safe, even the last of Two Twists' junior warriors had joined the main battle, eager for their first coup feather.

With their eyes fixed to the battle due east, those left in camp did not notice Iron Eyes and his force until they were swooping into the camp behind them and an old man shouted the alarm.

Their speed and agility were incredible. Arrow Keeper watched a Comanche brave lean far away from his pony and expertly scoop up a small child who was running toward a tipi, screaming. Another bore down on a young woman of about 16 winters and whisked her up onto the horse with him. He tapped her with his skull-cracker to subdue her fierce fighting.

Arrow Keeper lifted the .34-caliber British trade rifle he was carrying and fired, but his aim was off and his bullet flew wide. Besides, the Comanches moved so quickly it was nearly impossible to draw a good bead on them.

Instead, he gathered up two small children and broke for the cover of a tipi, tossing them inside. He rushed back out and encountered an old woman too stunned to move. The Comanches were not kidnapping elders, but already they had shot a few. She too he pushed to safety inside the tipi, ordering her to hold the children still.

Despite the lightning speed of the surprise assault, many in camp fought fiercely. One Comanche had been knocked soundly from his horse when a woman from the Eagle Clan swung on him with a wooden war club. But he leaped back on top of his spotted pony, whirled it around, and smashed the woman's skull so hard with his stone-cracker that Arrow Keeper heard the bone split like a walnut shell. A moment later the shrieking, drunk Comanche had scooped up a screaming girl.

He ripped off her clothing as he raced back toward the canyon, exulting in fierce, high-pitched cries. Arrow Keeper lunged toward a fallen elder and picked up another rifle. He hoped to at least drop the enemy's horse and give the girl a chance to escape on foot. But as he sighted on the Comanche's horse, another Comanche flew past closer at hand and kicked the old man hard in the skull with his stiff cavalry boot. Arrow Keeper dropped as if he'd been poleaxed.

Miraculously, Honey Eater had been missed in all the excitement. Now the main body of Comanche raiders was heading back for the canyon escape route, clutching captured children and young women. But Iron Eyes, still full of the scouts' report, had remained behind just to spot her. And now, despite the swirling dust, he lived up to his name, catching sight of a beautiful girl as she herded some crying children toward a tipi.

He wore spurs of Mexican silver. Now he gave sharp rowel tips to his horse, bearing down on the girl. His pistol cracked once and a boy was knocked to the ground, blood squirting in a high arc from a hole over his right ear. He fired again and a little girl screamed piteously when the slug lodged in her groin.

Comanche Raid

Honey Eater watched both children die before her eyes. She swept the others behind her and started to run, herding them like a prairie hen with chicks fleeing before a windstorm. The ground pounded behind her, and a child looked back and screamed, his eyes like huge black watermelon seeds in his fright.

Honey Eater too started to turn her head. A moment later she felt strong hands grip her under both arms and swing her up onto horseback.

Her suicide knife was already in her hand, but now it wasn't meant for her—not so long as a fight with child-killers was possible. She lashed out hard over one shoulder, slashing the Comanche war leader's face and almost breaking free of his grip.

Again she drew back her arm to cut him. A heartbeat later the steel butt of his pistol slammed into her temple, and she went slack.

The rest rode back to grim news: six elders and children had been slain, a dozen more wounded. More than 20 women and children were missing. Pursuit was out of the question—their ponies were exhausted from the double exertion of the hunt and the running battle. Nor could any strangers ever hope to outrun such excellent horsemen in their own country. One scout, River of Winds, was sent to follow them and blaze a trail.

And there could be no question what fate awaited the captives. Some would be tortured, no doubt, but not enough to mar their looks. They were intended for lives of degradation and slavery among Mexicans and palefaces.

An emergency council would be meeting even

167

Judd Cole

before the butchering and skinning of the kill and
the return to their permanent summer camp on
the Powder. But though he would attend like all
the other warriors, Touch the Sky's mind was
made up.

He was on his own now.

A door deep down inside of him had closed,
finally and permanently, on any hope of con-
ciliating his enemies to avoid sullying the Arrows.
Cooperation with the likes of Black Elk, Wolf Who
Hunts Smiling, and Swift Canoe was impossible.
Now he was *for* any one of them who dared cross
him, and this new readiness to kill was clear in
his eyes, which ran from no man.

His carelessness had allowed Honey Eater and
the others to be taken. Little Horse and Two
Twists constantly reminded him that they too had
failed to look for a second band of Comanche.
But Touch the Sky could not shake his sense of
guilt, his sense that this time he had truly failed
the tribe.

"Black Elk thunders to his troop brothers,"
Little Horse said as they met for the upcoming
council. "He boasts that no Comanche or Kiowa
dog will rut on his wife, that he will string their
hides from his lodgepole the way they hang up
roadrunner skins. At one time I admired him,
brother. I thought he was straight-arrow, but I
see now that he holds himself above the Arrows
as does his cousin."

But it was Arrow Keeper who saw the situation
as clearly as Touch the Sky did. He took his assistant aside before the meeting of the Headmen and
warriors.

"You know," he said, "that the crisis is coming

to a head? That you will soon be forced to kill or be killed even within your own tribe?"

Touch the Sky nodded. But with Honey Eater a prisoner, her fate at this very moment unknown, revenge against his tribal enemies was a remote thought.

"You have done your best to avoid it. Now, they have beaten you, tried to kill you for an elk, and tricked you into setting up a pole. You have atoned one time too many for the fact that you were raised by palefaces."

"Truly, Father. But I'm done with apologies and shame. I no more chose my place than that red-tailed hawk there by the river chose his. And Father, we both know that in Black Elk's case it is not my past with white men which makes him keen to kill me."

It was Arrow Keeper's turn to nod. The entire right side of his face was swollen and bruised from the kick which had knocked him out during the raid.

"You have tried the peace road. Now your mind is swollen with thoughts of rescuing Honey Eater and the others. In your distraction, your enemies will move against you again. Do you see that it is time, once again, to separate yourself from the tribe? That this thing must be done yourself?"

Touch the Sky had already concluded the same thing. He would listen to the council, would show no disrespect. But from here on out, he rode alone and followed no man unless he chose to. They had marked him as an outsider, punished him as one. Then so be it. He would act like one.

His heart was in an agony of loss over Honey

Eater. But in that same heart he vowed silently that between them was a genuine love which gave *him*, not Black Elk, a husband's right and obligation.

If others would ride with him, fine. If not, he would ride alone. He belonged to no clan, no soldier society, and was said to have the stink which scared away the buffalo. But who among them could also say he feared any warrior?

Yes, he had a husband's right and a warrior's pride and strength and courage. He would track his enemies into the very heart of their stronghold. One way or another he would rescue Honey Eater and the others. And *any* man who interfered—including any Cheyenne—would be killed.

CHEYENNE

JUDD COLE

Follow the adventures of Touch the Sky as he searches for a world he can call his own!

#1: Arrow Keeper. Born Indian, raised white, Touch the Sky longs to find his place among his own people. But he will need a warrior's courage, strength, and skill to battle the enemies who would rather see him die than call him brother.
___3312-7 $3.50 US/$4.50 CAN

#2: Death Chant. Feared and despised by his tribe, Touch the Sky must prove his loyalty to the Cheyenne before they will accept him. And when the death chant arises, he knows if he fails he will not die alone.
___3337-2 $3.50 US/$4.50 CAN

CHEYENNE

JUDD COLE

Follow the adventures of Touch the Sky as he searches for a world he can call his own!

#3: Renegade Justice. When his adopted white parents fall victim to a gang of ruthless outlaws, Touch the Sky swears to save them—even if it means losing the trust he has risked his life to win from the Cheyenne.
_3385-2 $3.50 US/$4.50 CAN

#4: Vision Quest. While seeking a mystical sign from the Great Spirit, Touch the Sky is relentlessly pursued by his enemies. But the young brave will battle any peril that stands between him and the vision of his destiny.
_3411-5 $3.50 US/$4.50 CAN

Two Classic Westerns
In One Rip-roaring Volume!
A $7.00 Value For Only 4.50!

"These Westerns are written by the hand of a master!"
—New York *Times*

LAST TRAIN FROM GUN HILL/THE BORDER GUIDON
_3361-5 $4.50

BARRANCA/JACK OF SPADES
_3384-4 $4.50

BRASADA/BLOOD JUSTICE
_3410-7 $4.50

LEISURE BOOKS
ATTN: Order Department
276 5th Avenue, New York, NY 10001

Please add $1.50 for shipping and handling for the first book and $.35 for each book thereafter. PA., N.Y.S. and N.Y.C. residents, please add appropriate sales tax. No cash, stamps, or C.O.D.s. All orders shipped within 6 weeks via postal service book rate. Canadian orders require $2.00 extra postage and must be paid in U.S. dollars through a U.S. banking facility.

Name _____

Address _____

City _____ State _____ Zip _____

I have enclosed $_____ in payment for the checked book(s). Payment <u>must</u> accompany all orders. ☐ Please send a free catalog.

WILDERNESS

GIANT SPECIAL EDITION:
SEASON OF THE WARRIOR

By David Thompson
Tough mountain men, proud Indians, and an America that was wild and free—authentic frontier adventure during America's Black Powder Days.

The savage, unmapped territory west of the Mississippi presents constant challenges to anyone who dares to venture into it. And when a group of English travelers journey into the Rockies, they have no defense against the fierce Indians, deadly beasts, and hostile elements. If Nate and his friend Shakespeare McNair can't save them, the young adventurers will suffer unimaginable pain before facing certain death.

_3449-2 $4.50 US/$5.50 CAN

WILDERNESS

By David Thompson

*Tough mountain men, proud Indians, and an America
that was wild and free—authentic frontier adventure
set in America's black powder days.*

#12: Apache Blood. When Nate and his family travel to the
southern Rockies, bloodthirsty Apache warriors kidnap his
wife and son. With the help of his friend Shakespeare
McNair, Nate will save his loved ones—or pay the ultimate
price.
_3374-7 $3.50 US/$4.50 CAN

#13: Mountain Manhunt. When Nate frees Solomon Cain
from an Indian death trap, the apparently innocent man
repays Nate's kindness by leaving him stranded in the wilds.
Only with the help of a Ute brave can Nate set right the
mistake he has made.
_3396-8 $3.50 US/$4.50 CAN

#14: Tenderfoot. To protect their families, Nate King and
other settlers have taught their sons the skills that will help
them survive. But young Zach King is still a tenderfoot when
vicious Indians capture his father. If Zach hasn't learned his
lessons well, Nate's only hope will be a quick death.
_3422-0 $3.50 US/$4.50 CAN